BLACK MASKS

BLACK MASKS

John Fraser

AESOP Modern
Oxford

AESOP Modern
An imprint of AESOP Publications
Martin Noble Editorial / AESOP
28 Abberbury Road, Oxford OX4 4ES, UK
www.aesopbooks.com

First hardback edition published by AESOP Publications
Copyright (c) 2009 John Fraser

First paperback edition published by AESOP Publications
Copyright (c) 2014 John Fraser

www.johnfraser.info

Yes, I Do like Brahms was first published in
the *London Magazine*, Sep.–Oct. 1989.

Parts of **The River** appeared in *Janiculum*,
first published by Edizioni Lupo, Rome, 1983.

ISBN: 978-0-9927588-2-0

Contents

'YES, I DO LIKE BRAHMS'

I ASSURED, I reassured my uncle. Who used to wear full Highland dress around the house, his eyes glinting for deer in the front garden: his ghillie's spyglass is on my table now, from Dixey's of New Bond Street. An instrument of infinite extension, but through which, for many years, I have seen – nothing.

'Uncle,' I would ask, 'tell me of your memories of something that didn't happen to you.'

And he would tell me of his days with the Red Cavalry, of herding buffalo, dressed in leather and with a long wooden lance, in the swamps of the Maremma. Then we would go and play together on his old Winkler grand, bought new in Dresden during the great devaluation.

'Not so much as a pair of trousers, this cost,' he would say, twirling the controls on the double piano seat.

We used to play Brahms's *Autumn Landscapes*, lullabies of his grief, or sorrow – or was it pain at all?

'Can I play the wolf notes, Uncle?' And I'd try to keep the left hand full of sound, full as the grapes in the Salzkammergut as Brahms must have seen them, as he walked about, trying to find his appetite for lunch, and dinner.

'Brahms was a one for salmon mousse,' said my uncle, making his deadfish eye. 'Keep on the wolf notes – I'm feeling that sabre cut in my left knuckles.'

And I toiled and rolled away.

Uncle was worried about the Great Crash. How it always came back, never bottomed out.

'Will you get a pair of trousers for the Winkler?' I asked, faux naif. I remembered what had happened to the Winkler factory – carried off to the East, what was left. And when I got to my room, I clipped my coupons for a silk shirt with flared cuffs.

My father was away fighting, perhaps for his life, perhaps for something more precious, like Brahms fighting for his liver. He sent me postcards – postcards he had not posted himself, perhaps not even written – with big, bright stamps. The stamps were bigger than the message Always from the 'Landscape' series – spring and autumn. Perhaps buying himself two packs of postcards when he had arrived. Seeking out the postcard tout, doing a deal, bleary off the train. Bottoming out. Noble tramp. Expensive bundle.

Brahms was the last one to have real experiences, eat real salmon, grow real cancer spores. 'Imagine,' I tried to thrill my listless uncle, 'he actually *wrote* classical music.' My uncle looked bored. 'Gave me a little case he had, for schnapps. Drank in the afternoons. Cried. A melancholy man.' He did not add that Brahms bored him, sailing like a maudlin swan on heavy oil-paint ponds, amidst the most beautiful convolvulus there's ever been.

'Yes,' said my uncle, 'perfect in his way.'

Perhaps Brahms would have gone on to play in the jazz combo, first delicately for the tea-dances, then madly, moussed with schnapps, seizing the trumpet's bowler-hat mute and cakewalking on the Sachertort. And by this time, quite, quite black.

Transmuted, turned into a postage-stamp like my father, who'd ask, 'Who now remembers Adenauer?' He'd loved the old man. If Adenauer had died and just become a corpse, my father would have taken mementoes, planted them like forest lines wherever he went. A sprig of Heimat, pines along the Tigris, saddlebags made of Konrad's eye-pouches.

'Don't trivialise,' snapped my uncle, as I dragged out the wolf' notes. 'Repetition must always improve on the first time. That way nothing is ever the same twice, but much much longer, or shorter. Or a different colour, or happier, a different nationality. An upward path to perfection.'

I thought of Brahms toiling upwards for his tea and the Kaiserin Elisabeth Hotel. Popping black bombers with the grooms, sniffing it up in the intervals at the English Tea Rooms. 'I dedicate these lines to my faithful horse Athos', wrote Count Stahremberg, winner of the Berlin–Vienna dash – that is, his horse was the winner, black and perfect in his way – and five short years later, Brahms was dead. At least, *that* Brahms; perhaps all of them – volley of shots over the grave, masked honour party – a wreath from old Harlem, a black funeral cake from the Winkler Piano Co.

Uncle had never recovered from the Depression, his great depression. On the other hand, my father's postcards came to an end. Perhaps he too, somewhere in Africa: turned blue, or simply walking off, into our destiny, following that high, rooty-tooting Brahms – black as his clarinet, weaving through the dunes like a sand-devil. Making that thing *sing*, and a farewell to melancholy.

Though not, it seemed, my uncle's.

THE RIVER

Yo soy el río que canta
al mediodía y a los
hombres,
que canta ante sus
tumbas,
el que vuelve su rostro
ante los cauces sagrados.

from El Río, Javier Heraud,[1]
for 15th May 1963

Vsevolod

THE RIVER

I AM WHITE – lying on white sheets staring at the ice-white ceiling. Outside there must be snow – it comes back through the window to me. There's a spray of waxy red flowers, like sparks of lantern: apple-wax on the floors that I can't see. I remember those broad rivers in the taiga, the banks pale as egg-yolks with mimosa, here and there smudged with frost like rust-blood specks of dead fertility. Out into the slow waters, staring into the pale sunset, pale as egg-yolk. And the frost would come, freeze the current, freeze the fishermen in the floe – float them

---

[1] Javier Heraud, Peruvian poet, was killed by police on the Madre de Dios river on this date. He was unarmed, and had been on his way to start a revolutionary foco.

down in the morning spate, dead, white. Only a few freckles dim through the hoar-frost – lantern-shapes, sickle-shapes: the moon pale as a yolk, and the pale lantern of morning sun, ornament between the white sheets of snow and the Chinese-white of the sky. The fishermen lying like husked almonds under a bowl with two pale symbols – or pale, pale cigars – a corpse wrapped in pale cigar-leaves launched into the morning spate, waking, as the colours deepen, to the jaguar and the mimosa. The jaguar pale as a cigar leaf and dark as almond husk. The jaguar, heavy with its own story, thinks, and slowly dips its dark tail towards the Chinese-white – inscribes a character upon that other river.

Heavy with my story, under the branch, I smell the rasp of cat-smell: 'the third river is always that of death'.

GROWING

HOW SLOWLY and grudgingly I came into the life of mankind, how grudgingly had I lingered over the taste of my marrow – a spoonful at a time – first the red caviar, then the black. Like a swimmer lowering himself from a branch, like a jaguar lying over the cooling current, or a fisherman settling into his boat, easing it into the stream, running the lines over his lined palm. People like me – who approach the new with diffidence and mistrust, resenting the old for its legacy of effeteness: who know that their sensibility was licked off other people's lives, like the sugar off a sugar-plum, replaced craftily in granny's box. Later, the family watching as my guilt was discovered, and I had to eat it, dark and fluffed-out with dust.

My God! We even knew the taste of guilt! How long before I could pull a fish from my river, look it in the eye and not see sugar-plums? Plump little boy – as the fashion was – gaseous, troubled with athlete's foot – though not performance.

'I want to join the Bolsheviks' – how could I come to say that, at least without examinations and tests to steel me? My aunt had her voluntary work, Gleb the coachman had a wooden leg and the promise of another if the cold split it as he drove aunt to her committees ... What was wrong with being a liberal, trusting the peasant soul as one trusts a mattress of goosedown? Why not wait for Herr Hartmann's locomotive to take me ('service before everything') to a provincial school – turning the merchant's son away from commerce, towards languor ...

I had been in uniform since I was old enough to know that after all there were other beings like me ... I remember Anatol saying to me, 'It's fine for you Russians – you'll be

free when the Tsar's dead – we will have to wait till we're
not Jews any more ... '

FAMILY HAPPINESS

MY AUNT talked of morphology, though the colours never
deepened in her room – a brown cat playing with its tail, a
samovar of white metal, the unread French novels yellowing
like mimosa – and I, little Vsevolod, whom she called the
'idiot of the family', butt of her boredom, watching the
mimosa-yellow globes bubbling under the dead-white
cornices of the drawing-room, the brown cat playing with
little globes that fringed aunt's shawl – dreaming of
jaguars...

SHOOTING

THEY LOOK like partridges themselves, down-soft English jackets the colour of bracken, peaked caps blindly scanning for mother's return. Bang, bang – passing along the line, a cruel spoof, like grandmother's picture of dead hunters buried by their prey – the boars grinning. I am standing there, dressed as a little boy, holding Miss Bookinyum's hand – I remember only her hand, her name softened and rounded as I liked it ... How often she thrust those steely English syllables into my jaws, like a curb, pressing down my tongue when it was sugar-plums I wanted. I am standing in my biography, remembering the snails curled like tabbies in the ferns. The smell of cordite, pigeon's blood: blood on the breast feathers reminds me of my uncle's purple greatcoat. His shiny boots carried him back to us – killed, they told me, at the Front. Where else should a soldier die, I thought, but smashed in at the chest, or with a single pellet-hole through which his memory leaked out, blood spilling like celluloid falling away from the spool? When these hunters went to war, I thought of their bodies, soft and warm in piles: a pleasant accumulation, counted and marvelled over by Yuri the loader ... 'Come along now – little boys shouldn't spend too long with dead animals.' This, my earliest memory, is the last tableau I've contrived. I hid the snails, the pink cardboard of the cartridges, little clots of authenticity like chocolate-flakes, quartzes in a load of gravel ... Yes, here I am, I recognise myself: my Norfolk jacket – 'Norfolk is a province by the sea', – like Lapland, Miss Bookinyum milking reindeer. I hid these fossils for myself to find: standing solemn in the sepia light, played hide-and-seek to guarantee my future. My past is buried like

a city, ordered, persistent as syntax. Below the lowest level
– clay.

EDUCATION

THE SUN struggling in the evening haze, like a golden fish slowly wrestled to the shoreline, reminded me of my childhood, of the muddy deaths of winter, of the ominous coming of spring, of the new knowledge already stored in the heads and the sticks of my teachers – some of it sharp, pointed, rigorous, like the knuckle-rapper of Shterner, the mathematician – some of it ill-formed, ungainly, like the lath still covered with plaster which Volkov used to chalk our backs ... How I grew to hate those overstuffed categories of the bourgeoisie – they were like my aunt's Chesterfields, tufted with hair that could be human, spotted with ink and bound in bookman's calf. How to escape from what the adults already knew – how, when one was small and could not run fast, could I escape those intellectual sticks? I longed for books with blank pages, but my family, to economise, made me use textbooks whose margins were cluttered with the fumbling errors of my predecessors – commentaries on commentaries – every printed paragraph eagerly appended with sycophantic manuscript agreement, some young mind anxious to suggest still more examples to the pedant who'd managed to steal my time long after he'd entombed his own in these foxy pages.

GREAT MUDHOLE

MARX AND ENGELS looking for new science in the bosom of the old society – so I too, tiring of the bosoms of old society, wandered down the avenues of constituted reality, watching the old soldiers, their greatcoats grey as dust, shuffle past the new subalterns – their coats with a tinge of purple showing through, like plum flesh under the bloom. Natasha's pink tongue lic7king reality like ice-cream: keep at it, little girl, it will soon all be gone.

... it was odd to have made a revolution, and to be hated. Even people who should have flocked to Robespierre and cheered the tumbrils thought us the most disagreeable and disgraceful fellows. Some hated us because we'd changed the names of things. I saw people who knew the city from childhood standing puzzled on street corners – 'Why now – this used to be Ekaterinskaia: who's this fellow they've put up in its place? Who's crazy here? Did I take the wrong turn? ... '

How everything hurt in those days. Overnight, everyone in Russia had forgotten how to make boots: all they could make was blisters. You'd have thought policemen had never been seen in the empire before, there was such a fuss ... And in the midst of it, we Bolsheviks strode – huge strides – freeing the slaves, emancipating this, stopping that, organising the people of regions so huge and so distant they didn't even know where they lived ... and all the while, more and more people clinging to our coat-tails, slowing us down. I myself was quite exhausted when they sent me to the fishermen. On the cart that took me there, I designed a canning factory, a big fishing collective, and a station for marine biology. You could tell where the village began: the ruts in the road became the channels of an estuary. The rich peasants kept dogs in their boats to bark at the poor peasants who ate the fish scraps the others dropped to their animals. Most of the villagers never went out into the current in their boats – which were too rotten to be trusted: they threw lines from their houses into the mud: the stranded eels were glad enough for a snap at the after-life. The dogs barked to each other all day – they were the intellectuals of the place ... bow-wow about summed up the place anyway.

Sometimes the fishermen would swap fish for vegetables if someone with a cartload happened to be passing, but neither side was excited enough by the transaction to maintain it on a regular basis. Across the bay, there were fine sites for houses – but the men had sold their axes to buy hooks when they first built the village. Upstream the mimosa hung in the fog, like drops of congealed sunlight. Where the river was narrower, they could have set fish traps, or lines across the river. But their life in the mud was living witness to their religion, its message of submission to the worst that nature could devise. Sometimes they would gather together and sing what must have been versions of hymns – sylvan modes predominated. Perhaps they'd been forest dwellers, so feckless they burned down their home. At times, the men would try to carve the supports of their houses into crude totems, but the wood was rotted through, and the whole structure was endangered.

Why had these people let nature defeat them so decisively? 'We would rather be victims of nature than of other men,' they said. 'We prefer to escape the slavery of men by being enslaved to nature,' they said. 'We have our pride ... '

SPRING IN GREAT MUDHOLE

... and yet, I remember another people – sacrificing themselves like polyps so that their reef would rise above the sea, support higher forms of life, and themselves becoming higher with the sacrifice. In order to die as a human being, you have to have lived as one.

The villagers were reassured that the mud would liquefy: would wrinkle, harden and crack like parched elephants' skin, would turn again to liquid and then freeze. The mud wasn't going anywhere and neither were they. The mud was an admirable, even a philosophical, presentation of their own condition.

But at least they had the good grace to be miserable without the services of intellectuals – unless, as I've said, you count the dogs. They had legends, but did not much enjoy them. They apologised for telling them. But no one felt it necessary to have poets, astronomers, playwrights, printers' devils, soubrettes, promoters, society prize-fighters – to express their desires. If anyone had a desire, he expressed it immediately – by drifting on the current out of sight of Great Mudhole – perhaps to freeze to death, who knew? The village existed before desire and outside hypocrisy.

At the end of three months, I had imported only one significant expression of man's profoundest need – a red flag which I flew from the ridge-pole of my hut. For a time it seemed to be bleaching pink, but then some reaction in the dye took hold. I feared the village would soon be sailing under the black flag of anarchy, where it belonged ...

But I myself was at fault: I did not know these people. They could have been pine-trees for all I knew of them. They nicknamed me 'The Detonator' – but when mud is aroused, it just falls back into place – only the detonator is no more.

And yet – I had to get this place moving ...

THE CAT

HER TAIL floats like a feather in the ruined garden: loosestrife, mallow, hollyhock, survive before the denser dwarf-wood takes over. Her feather – one of exploration – intuitive, empirical, but unassuming. Writing from the nose – a prose that will not take in this wetness, sliding from hillock to puddle, a watery ink – characters blurred and swollen, like black twigs, newts or turds dropped in water ...

ALEKSANDRA

ALEKSANDRA – how she disembodied me: sleeping with me, she said, was like sleeping with the future; I was like a bill which became due only long after she would have worn out the merchandise.

Nature asserted itself in the ruins: the river mist washed out our horses' bodies like a film of silver on a photograph. Green weeds, stuffed with red berries like a salmon's roe, stood sharp in the tumbled thatch. The copper plates on the dome of the church had burst away from their frame, clanging Roman armour with every languid motion of the mist. Everywhere water – the horses breathed out spume, the reins were heavy as the strings on a fishing net: we came slowly down the main street, like drowning sailors struggling their way down into Atlantis ...

The grass was silver, the walls of the biggest house blue, grey, purple, the skin of a man scorched with gunpowder. The fire had swept through the lilac and syringa in front of the house, flattened their colours on the plaster ...

How frightened Aleksandra was to see us, wet and hairy as otters, coming to take a bite of her soft flank! 'Hey, little salmon,' someone shouted, 'swim to shore with me!' Strange, how that first gesture, that movement between flight and question, should have summarised our time together, the mist cutting us off.

Like the jaguar I remember on that other river, sitting on its invisible bough above the mist, floating in one dimension while I floated past him in two. What a trick she had of looking past me – she thought all the Reds were common fellows, mechanics, shoemakers, drunken peasants: she never understood why the Whites would burn the town – it just made us seem the worse. How delicate to introduce myself to this strangeness, who could be my cousin ...

CHORDS

THE PIANO repeated six bars over and over through the hazy afternoon fields, the notes intense, distorted by the columns of hot dust rising tall as poplars. It was early summer, and we peered through the heat like half-blind artisans looking at life through their mica windows ... Soldiers were drilling: you could see the distant ranks incline, turn from grey to plum to purple as the light caught the planes. Then, the orders – coming slowly and indistinctly, as falsetto comment on the movements already executed. The piano caught a phrase in proper time – repeated it, wrongly. It was early summer: only the mice had hopes for the harvest – the wheat was green and sour. I oiled our typewriter and wrote 'Lontano' ... the sound of the typing startled us, it was so even and synchronous. 'Praise God,' said someone, 'here come tomorrow's orders. No sooner has he oiled the typewriter than he write orders with it. No sooner cleaned his gun, he shoots it at some poor idiot.'

Far away the little wedges of infantry anticipated the feeble voices of their officers and started to march towards the village. The piano stopped – a cicada numbed to silence by the first chill of the night. We all knew the front would be breached at dawn, and we looked at the wheat-fields, thinking of our bodies ripening there all summer: war, land, bread. So long as there was someone left to make the harvest ...

Mary-Lou

SPRING IN CANADA

IT'S SPRING again. The cat – Mike calls her 'Butch' – grabs
the doorposts, scampers. I approach Mike through the cat –
she licks herself down after each exertion, paws and
shoulders, hunts the paper, more assiduous than any
archivist. Those old communists, grandfather's friends –
they pride themselves so on living. They have it all
straightened out: you agree with someone else's life. Or
rather: my own existence doesn't convince me: it is to them
I shall come back. The cat sits, ears short, cropped almost.
Mike gets in between us, a good man, fallen amongst the
obdurate. How he hates a verbal subtlety, even when it
conceals a compromise. He hates principle – it means the
end of us both.

It's spring: the trees that haven't made it still carry last
year's berries through. It's too early yet for leaves – this
white room, where each day I'm left, engraved with spider
lines, victories over each day – *l'art d'ennuyer* ... And the
movement from the novel, from the frozen to the real. Is it
really through the thaw that one makes the crossing, mud
held together with grassroots?

One ear ginger and one white, a grey, wrinkled forehead
– and every night Mike returns, silent about his triumphs,
defeated there, and here at the point of reproduction. The cat
stands at the window, dreaming of Isfahan. That grey
forehead, wrinkled with doubts; and every night Mike
stands at the window watching nothing, impatient with the
darkness ... How he longs to paint this room – as though he
sees conclusions engraved, extended beyond the lines of the
plasterer's trowel – to paint away my dead knowledge, the

paintbrush loaded against the orgy ... Mike buries himself; he enjoys the exertion, the finality – even the dutiful tear.

My white room, tracked with winter: the cat purrs snottily under my chair, and outside a pump, or a cicada, re-opens the beetle tracks to mud and dissolution. It is the thaw – and Mike and I cling to snow and ice.

GRANDFATHER

... and upstairs lies my sly grandfather. Did he run or did he slide? What stories he has to fill those twenty years, those years when the hoofbeats swept him downstream. It's right that he educates me by making me a fiction – a Nadezhda, a Mary-Lou: if I follow his story I arrive only at his artifice, his wink. He's a great pedagogue – he leads one only to questions.

Those twenty years – the years of the shades, he calls them: but still, the shades had a fine big army. For him, it was like reincarnation – he to the lower, the shades to concreteness. Too old to start again, and by dying: he is empty, a prisoner of the stream. What did he do for twenty years, forgetting if he left in defeat or in success? How easily they must have passed, those years beyond loyalty, beyond effort, beyond the dogs of Mudhole. Haven't you seen them – the kulaks and commissars in carpet slippers, secure in the truce of Joe's Diner? And we – what, basmachi? Speaking to each other the language slaves use to their masters, that bitterness that becomes inflection, frustration a grammar, we in this city where we have no language to express our hatred...

Vsevolod

THE FUNCTIONARY

STICKS OF the teasel – a fine tool – and two lambs' heads, dusty brown curls unpatched from the simple bone, fragments of my old indolence. Here I lie under the bridge, boots aloft, the leather responsive to the curious toe, and round me lie the shavings from the factory floor, the nervous teasels and the lambs whose dried tongues seek the missing gums ... So many histories I lived through, to have seen it all, caught it all in the religious egotism of the word ... But, loving myself too much, I have become the narcissus of the pebble beach, admiring multiplicity as myself, and I transcend each stone by my similarity to its brother. My double – don't be reassured by our resemblance: a pebble beach is not like rock or clay – it can't be worked upon by water. Either it's clay that has decided to take itself in hand, or boulders in second childhood.

Above me is a crack, and the arch will let the frost in and in the spring the bridge will fall. The workers are coming home across the fields: they call me 'mister', and some 'mister-comrade'. Here lie the stolen lambs' bones, here the illicit flax – and here I lie, not in complicity, but indolence. I have come through, I have succeeded and become – too little. With discipline I ended pliant as a pickled rod: I fear the judgment of the hard ones who must take things on – hard as I once was, but just. Yes, I have lost justice – I cannot decide the conditions of my life.

WAR

OUR SEMINARISTS were not spoiled, but terminated: they talk often of the hand of God, but seldom of the foot. I have a chronology, but not a biography – or rather, Mary-Lou, I was dying when you first met me, and so minute by minute I live again. But guilt for Mary-Lou-Nadezhda, outweighed by Aleksandra, is just a convenience: she's so far only a course of events, kicks and squeals, that needs no pity and no reason outside herself and those who love her.

Of course, we had great intellectuals, who were profoundly reactionary: we discussed this endlessly, and we were big men, you understand. My choice was prison, death, desertion: but really all of these at once or none. We knew our time was up when they sent noodles. Pavel said, 'They always send the noodles when a town's about to fall.' So while the lads die about us we'll slip through the lines, to that desolation over the river ...

It's always our great men who want to finish the last century: I agree we must be tidy. What, after all, is your suffering worth when you're dead? But even in Great Mudhole we weren't stupid: nothing fooled us, except the fish, swimming up-river. I always had this snout for life, like pussy sniffing in the garden – and I was lucky, I knew them across the desk and in the office, and when they threatened me I knew the thing to say. Well, well: sorrow for all that's left. Unless it's to be done again, but facing faceless nothing a thousand times means I didn't want it all again...

Winter dips its crusts in the river, and day by day is greedier. Our general is having trouble, used to retreats on four legs. All this lumber to pick up and take back, it worries him. Our workers are dying there while he stands embarrassed at the telephone: 'What does it mean, no contact on the flank – no telephone or no Germans?'

I've talked to those who will resist: some friends of Aleksandra, women who can live rough and be trained meanwhile. The men are all too soft: I don't like ascetics, but the others have no discipline. Some of the best are missing: some are coming from the camps, but not enough. I've seen men come straight from interrogation to the front – but the soldiers are troubled, and the commissars don't know what to say. They're worried by the workers, and the peasants: with party men and office workers – there they can say their piece and score their points.

Noodles: for the emperor, before the fascists come, and we shall cross the river, into the after-death, a land sour with mortality, into the land of vulgar materialism, tree-stumps and my comrades' blood. It is the land of the plague-dream, the silence of the incubus. They lie outside the cottages: and some still sit, disciplined, in the trucks. But this too is a battlefield, and we see them where the camera stopped, already the fierce brows greyed-in with crusts of snow ...

Mary-Lou

DREAM

A RADIO that gives out obolonga fruit and tenderloin and lets you talk to astronauts – but can't be turned off. 'Why would you want to turn off a radio that gives out obolonga fruit?'

'Magic garden: entrance $5'.

Formalists discussing the length of sentences in prison.

What to do, in this city of Mount-Royal, a city in which we have not yet begun to live, in which our suffering is cold and repetitious, ice-chips on the glacier. What expenses, what deserts, what ice-fields of time before us! Our crises, our tempers, our strikes, our manifestoes – forgettable as melodramas, slave-acting in the lower depths of this city ... A city where we drive to labour, our cars like shuttles in a huge loom making continents of grey cloth. How can I say I live, member of a class which does not live – or lives as an arm lives, as a horse lives, as an officer of the court lives.

To marry Michael is to step into the abstract – an intelligence which refuses to use itself. 'To be as self-sufficient as you are is a crime against humanity,' he tells me. And I agree. It's a hard thing. When I talked to him of the city where we do not yet begin to live, I made a mistake and called it a city where we do not begin to think, and he laughed and said one lived first, then thought. But he doesn't think.

Mary-Lou and Mike

THE SAILOR crushed the crab's claw with his boot, showing us it was still alive. 'I can eat any one but that one' – and Mike, thinking in any case that it might be spoiled, agreed. But it was brought – 'from another country' – and tasted good.

'While the crab lived it kept the space between the shell and flesh lined with tears,' I thought, and said, 'We put to sea in a boat made of cardboard, and dare each wave to sink us.'

'That's OK then; cardboard doesn't sink.'

'But the box disintegrates—'

'Christ, enjoy the sun and the pleasure the crab gives you: Mrs. Jellyfish – that's the name I'll call you!'

Outside, the sun draws up crude slabs of glass, bushes of faience: full midday, when no one can see the sun, the heat comes, from below – that rocky forest underfoot, of sedimented gasoline and french-fries, walking perilously on liquid sand along the beach we go, claw in claw.

Vsevolod

ALEKSANDRA

AND WHAT a mistake was Aleksandra! The 'endless repetition of pettiness' which defined the best marriage, my friend Valerii said, became in our liaison a veritable glut of sour crabs from a virgin apple tree. Seeing pussy die made her convinced of immortality, and she pronounced on the death of fieldmice, Bolsheviks, bootmenders – all for the same suspended fee.

In those years, I had a friend, a train driver, who one day drove his 'iron steed' – he called it – unwittingly head-on into another. The boiler tapped him like a hammer. We lost so many at that time: they'd so few engines, to increase their output they raised the speed limits – enterprising in this case, ran two trains on a single track ... And poor Aleksandra, saved from the pathos of apostasy, wheeled her barrow, honourably, through the factory yard, until one day came to a sudden stop. Perhaps it was the wind perhaps the shock-workers didn't dig enough: the wall came, as you might say, like a ton of bricks. Poor Aleksandra: 'you tread but once the bridge that falls' – maybe, but Aleksandra passed by that wall a thousand times. The dust rose, puffy, arched: a nest of fieldfare's eggs lay unbroken. 'Send this to the cook at once! No, not to eat, to live!' She was remembered by her socks (the bricks had not begun to break up when they hit, and she was simply crushed, unmarked) – so thick they were, her fragile legs seemed equipped with charcoal claws, the boots burst, socks unravelling.

'So, the fine one goes.'

'Shhh, she was the director's bird!'

'Some job he gave her, then – she could have cooked his fieldfare's eggs!'

'But he's a strong one – and her boots, we've all got better. Now, about this wall, what did it do?'

'It stopped the smoke: it used to blow across the road. Comrade director, shall we start to build?'

I was grateful when Andrei said, 'Comrades, there will come a day when the death of any worker will be the cause of recriminations; a complaint that will stir the fears of labourers, not the overseer. Store up. your regrets by all means – but let's not make urgency turn us callous; nor calculate the loss of a comrade as less than that of personal friends. Aleksandra laboured humble: not, perhaps, as a socialist, but self-effaced, with no desire for privilege – no longing for the past, nor malice for the future.'

Well, any malice served her poorly and my excuses. But Andrei said to me, 'Now we can rely on you to do to generations what you tried with Aleksandra.'

'Really, is, that all you want? Something so little, and so cloying? *Madame, il fait grand vent et j'ai tué six loups* ... ? You have every trust in me, in my incompetence, in my ability to succeed only in the simplest things, to make another vigorous, and without hating me? You are too kind. Aleksandra dies of war wounds, drawn up to heaven in a question-mark of cordite ... What you ask is a thousand times heavier than my charity to her, a friendship, in the end, smoothed out by calculation ...'

Andrei hears only my talk of cordite, investigates for sabotage. We have so much of it, here in the country, here we feel hemmed in. Perhaps the wall was weakened in the night – thin watchmen whore, the fat ones sleep: and who last spoke of politics? Those old dry-bones in the engine-shed: they call me lackey, laugh when I turn away. So much the worse for them: Andrei gives the new pay-scales tomorrow, and they don't do well. Re-classified as common labourers. I agree: even to talk to them – they use their oil-cans as forefingers, their clothes are like the prologue's, covered with greasy tongues, the points of exclamation.

Aleksandra framed on my desk: what can I get from her? A new issue of socks all round, more lime for the cement. But no more. And no more even that friendship – she, waving from the mixer, and I winking as the local dealers (now we call them 'comrade') sell me their stuff – flanged noses flattened by the dealing finger, breath warm enough to warm the ministry stamp, carried, I now see, by the 'assistant'. One fox to hold the door and one to eat the chickens: those first lean foxes frighten me.

Making love in the photograph: the powder flash lights up the silver birches – a flight of ponies' legs, the silver so bright it makes the leather, leaves, seem purple. The cat, eager for her breakfast ('watch where you step, pussy') – grey and silver, makes the frame – and beyond the grove, where cockerels cluck like officer-cadets, the morning shells splash silver in the river. Preparations for breakfast: ten years later I, an honest though a lazy man, deal blindly with my thieving colleagues. The history's already written – the rogues are gone: only we honest ones are left. But as I sit here, my mistress's body, notched like a pike's with reeds, gills bloody, reproaches me. And not for larceny, but compromise: that 'mistress' comes so easily – and that at least she hated; that was 'the old way'.

Preparations for war: the brick dust off the desk. When am I saying this? Five years have passed, my bobbing cork eludes the stones, while thieves of thieves survive. Where are the visionaries, the Babel-looters? Not in the engine-shed. But, would you do it all again, if it happened all again? Wink solemnly. The historic present is a tidal soil – even acorns smell it out! But yes, I am a communist, and

knowing what I know I fight. Preparations for war:
Aleksandra was lucky. In Moscow there aren't enough
desks for each body in the first day of war. In the army I
used to say a man's worst friend is his mind, his best enemy
the rifle. The mind always hopes you're still alive – the rifle
is quick to give you up for dead ...

VILLAGE CONTACTS

SOME LANGUAGES fit one's needs like the skin on a tongue, like the saddle on a horse that has saved your life so often that it 'drinks a drop of your soul', as the cossacks said. When I talked to the girl, it seemed to me I had this universal language: when I spoke to her of the river, she could point to the inverted waves on the ceiling, silver on the white: 'That is our river, so close you could see it from the window.' Which language does not have its river, its terms for our common struggle?

And yet – I was so full of history, of knowledge – I am like the animal who curls up after a meal, snug in a warm cave, full of other animals, and 'tells' of its need for warmth, of a gentle death – in a million years – to the young archaeologists. Ah, to see that consciousness in their eyes, to see them struggling so desperately in the few years – the few years won from the cavalry, from my aunt's errands, from aesthetics – they have to appropriate all that knowledge. Even from the little shards of dog-existence on the cave floor.

I asked, 'And your people – do they struggle as mine did, as they will?' What language am I speaking – not a language of the state, surely, not a language of oppression – for it comes so easily to me. But geography – well, I know they have a river, but I can't see it. A language of production – well, no: I produce nothing. Say only, a language of fraternity?

But there are only the two of us. And yet, how different from when I began, hesitating between the red and the white like a card-player over a discard. Behind her voice I can hear others: people are working – reaping, making a raft, making defences for the village ... And perhaps behind my voice she hears the voices of those millions whose despair and whose strength shaped my sentences like chessmen. Before the battles we played chess ...

ALEKSANDRA

SO, FIGHTING each other, we passed the seasons. How impressed we were, Aleksandra and I, by the magnificent chestnut trees which dropped their three-toed leaves into the furrows in the road made by last spring's carriages. A wind from the east put the leaves and branches in mandarin conference: the white spires burnt out like fireworks.

'How distant I am from your comrades,' she said, 'and you – you who think so little of being a bourgeois ...'

'I shed my leaves to last the winter – who knows what flowers will come next spring? This year there's no fruit on the chestnuts – perhaps it's true, that these trees had some affinity with Antigone: they bear no fruit every seventh year, and the next – red spires. A child's tale, but one that concerns children, eh? – their games, such fierce loyalties, habits ...' I teased her.

'So much effort for so little meaning – why, any fool with a bottle of vodka puts more content in his stories than there is in any myth hawked around for a thousand years. A painter will work for a year to give you a picture of a man on a horse – why he's probably passed you a dozen times himself on horseback! We need stuff that will wake you up, not waste time in truisms and nursery anxieties.'

Aleksandra! I didn't realise you were in the full roar of the current, numbed by the cold, sweeping way under – I thought you were aloof, that we sparred as intellectuals. But no, you were half dead and half asleep. How poignant – that my words of encouragement to you were heard as funeral rites, your beauty – just flesh ... Your eyes, filling with water not their own – quickly, let go, or be dragged down with you ... Will you break the hold, or shall I? It's a problem solved in a second ...

SEASONS

ALEKSANDRA and I travelled into the country. The farms stood with their backs to the forest, their mica windows facing the fields and sun. The heat seemed to gather in the grey barnsides, scorch the red and brown halms. But it was winter still, peasants reclined on their wooden trucks and their horses ran swiftly over the frozen ruts of the backtracks. The trees were ice-coated, a little frail, trembling and unsteady like old aunts in new paste.

Before long, we saw ourselves, our friends, attacked in the newspapers. To have done so much that was wrong, but not venally, and to find suddenly that no accounting would be made of our real deficiencies ... As my assistant said, 'A real discussion follows – but you have to be there in person, or send a return envelope.'

That evening, there was a circus – 'We are all here, watching nonsense, but one we like' – people who do, and fail to do, what we might like to try. 'Being what I ain't,' I overhear someone say, 'a poet, and don't want to be neither ...' The animals lumber around the ring. Their straight lines and pauses painfully erased. How hard to learn a simple nonsense: round and round without pausing. We applaud them as they botch our simplest tricks, fall off the seesaw, fail to bite off the trainer's head. What fine fellows we are – the beasts stand in for our base slaves – before us, the ancient mode turns like a mill-wheel, and high in the roof the youths in white and purple tumble weightlessly.

THE SECOND WAR

AND SO it's war again – how far have we come? I see them
struggling with the oak roots. How deep do they run, these
tendrils that resist the axe? Men sleep criss-crossed with
roots, the trenches – should they try to take us here – fall
back and deep like mine-shafts. We practise dying every
day: but fighting against our enemies within, or designate,
we lack the realism which we long have lacked ... Not that I
enjoy that convention, that unfailing syntax: our activity
will affect you all – even that which, as old Herzen said, 'we
cannot put in novels' – or was it that he said, rather,
'laughter – is not always a sign of gaiety, or irony of
disillusion'? Now we shall show, foreign comrades, if your
fascism was tough, your bourgeoisie complacent. So –
you've got us into it: did you think capitulation would give
us the best chance? Did you give all you could, while every
paper told you we were having difficulties? Too late now:
not at the best time, but here we are – mattocks and axes
digging our first ten million graves ... Comrades – if only
you'd understood politics!

In thirty years will the Yanks still hunt their 'migrants'
across the deserts? Success with these axes will tell whether
in hundreds or in thousands.

'Comrades – you're digging tombs there – the back-up
trench must not slope back or one grenade will do for all!
And what will we do back there at all? Perhaps the second
wave waits for the next war? We need lines and lines –
stretching far back – the survivors ...' More opportunism.
He who fights and runs away objectively opposes mortality.
Materialists fight once, then it's back in the mineshaft.

I hear the Americans have a secret weapon: one says it is
the stick, another that it is the carrot. As I passed the village,

the hares were being taken out to execution: ominous, that. We'd no papers for a week, but the economy of private rabbits runs from Danzig to the Urals; radio, that finger aerial laid on those electric hearts ... 'So long-ears finds the price to pay – a broken neck on armistice-day ... '

Long-ears myself: so long they waited, and they got it wrong. We could have taken them in '21: but now, it takes steel to grind them down. I did my best: let the back-trench slope forward, and instead of Aleksandra's wall, a mound of earth – and on the top, some salty lupins where a hare may sit and watch the steel. Here at the crossroads stand the skinny wives, four ears in each hand. Our trucks go by: facing each other, clean hair, tall packs – who wants a rabbit in the front line? The women smile at me, superior: all war is the peasant war, except in England, and everywhere but there the victims kill their livestock and themselves wait, heads bowed, the brain ready for the killer's bolt.

Look at them all! Moscow must be empty! Even to cut their hair, press those uniforms ...

CROSSING THE RIVER

I AM in the dream again. We cross a raft of dead dogs, all pointing, frozen with their noses to the south. An army in retreat suffers like a pie before a seated glutton: a sudden movement in the gut and men die four deep in the ditches. At other times – the bigger the pie, the more the very sight inspires nausea.

Before we are beaten, we cross the lines. We can smoke, on this raft. There is so much play with the current, we can pole upstream and still land in our new country, our inverse land. The fascists have never known what it is to kill so many – their puritanism bites back: thank God for the enlightenment. They don't shell the dead dogs, or us, but dream instead of the parish – wife, dog, three kids, Mercedes, drunk on Saturday, sex and a sermon Sunday – and all in their favourite language. Not this brute we have – Masha at the bow, incomprehensible, with her fag, as she noses us back to the other shore. Poor Herzen – must be confused by now ...

On this side, frogs still yarp, Moscow accents – Masha smiles and, lugging explosives on the flats, thinks herself closer to home. The frogs are funny till we try to hop, hop, hop along this deep beach. The lines are slack here – and we crossed the other side when it was tired of hunting. They've killed so many of us ... through liking it, for most, and for the others, mathematics. Like their economics, they practise murder indiscriminately: the totality they like to squish – the family.

Up, over the bank with our big guns and what we hope is food. To live in exile, to live in this barren land. To know what we have lost, to have crossed the river, to have gone back – alas, as double agents, since the old man's so suspicious – to have crossed our ocean, starting again, knowing all we know. With the Party men they killed, they played sexy tricks: the Party women they were afraid of. Already we fill these woods with comradeship: I remember how those people across from Mudhole were – forest workers, threading through the trees like shuttles. Now, they are dead: and we who seek them become friends.

WOUNDED

TO LIVE and betray, or die and be forgotten ... How easily one forgets the point at which one left the battlefield. What last image did I trap before I plunged into the concrete, the world of others' experience – that tiny insentient instance, the break in the circle never again to revolve through consciousness ... ? What did I see before I became a fact for someone else – not a moral one, but a caponised bundle in the flux of someone's defeat?

Two old women licking up the goose-grease – grease for the sled's runners. I am lying here dead in the snow – give me an easy trundle, east or west. 'To read our greatest novel you must first acquire an understanding of French,' I said. They went on licking. Was this a year of victory or defeat? I can't remember. I feel lazy, wrapped in ice, my throat filled with cold blood. They are tugging me down a track as smooth as glass, smooth as a crystal catching the starshells, resounding with artillery like a crystal bowl booming to the connoisseur's finger. I am dead, and my journey is aesthetic, formal. The old women pant like horses. And I died, not knowing if in victory or in defeat, travelling on roads of frozen bodies – the glass so thick you could hardly see the fine uniforms. In that war, all the women became old. Between victory and defeat – only a few months, but between my youth and my old age a generation among the shades. I can't return, whether I betrayed the victory or the defeat. We are out in the current now – stamping and grunting down the frozen river, their hooves wrapped in rags. The runners whistle, breathless, as a woodsman whistles for the tree to fall, half cut through, its spring tense as a mile of ice. Crick, crack – you shouldn't have eaten the goosegrease.

THE CROSSING

CROSSING the river – like crossing into another year, another country: on the flats I can see seven birds, each of a different species, sniff out twice as many lichens ... Stuffed with noodles, I drop a word against the regional commander. Out here they've even killed the dogs – it's like Eden, only snakes and naked corpses – here we stand like colonists, no need to kill the Indians, some plague has done for them. How will we work here, where there is nothing?

We crossed the river, fighting its down-currents, like dark clouds across the stream, dark clouds across the moon, or where the moon should be ... Back we go to the future – safely to kill any man that moves: they wanted a desert and to rule it – so much the worse for them.

Mary-Lou

THE MASSACRE

GRANDFATHER'S troop, tiny under the pines, moving through wood engravings like the critical spirit ... First the bluebells, then the lupins – the salty blue swashes under the blue smoke –oatmeal smells of late autumn. A smattering of small animals –from the breakfast-table they're named, renamed. They – we – stand awkwardly, watch the valleys where the breakfast smoke shortly changes to black, productive. From the smoke, you can tell the seasons, and last year's weather. Only the dogs tell us we're at war – packed in but silent still, they run silent through these woods. The undergrowth is full of food. It is the moment before the fugue begins. The sea once seen lives and lives relentlessly. The oatmeal, catching at the edges, pricks behind the forehead ...

They climbed around the hill, spiralling, bent under their heavy guns, sweating above, their eyes on the mould, the nursery toadstools. An excursion always involuntary. I see them now, filing through the trees, at first on the path, padded feet denting, the holes filling with water. In the wood, the dead, the fallen trees: a smother of arms, distraught, a tree's gone down. They walk on, picking the husks of breakfast, tongues busy about the back teeth, familiar as the smell of boiling water – a pleasure. Politics, to them – like hygiene, a condition of the muscles. My sextant, grandfather, holds them sighted – trudges along.

The brambles are so pale here, the leaves yellow and spotted, here in the dark. Upward through the darkening forest they move, towards its broken edge, its deep chalk cliff. They saw where the massacre had been. It takes so many men to kill so many, and such concern about straight lines, counting, and standing still. A continuous process, not a final one at all – the last breath of the hunt; still there is movement. So much, too much, activity – this hollow where they kill us all, unfed, tires us with repetition, and if we live we can only snap, snap back at those lines of dogs. Snap, snap – but they have us in the guts. The sky is blue above their snouts, their jaws – and grandfather, powerless, looks from the edge, thinking of the boisterous play the dogs have with the dying hare, the hare that screams – seeing only the blue sky, saliva, flapping tongues. Below is the pain, and straight ahead that blue and penetrated sky.

Vsevolod

THE RIVER

DRAGONFLY. A lacquer ship, snagged in a sea of lacquer. By the other shore, beating against a contrary breeze, a second dragonfly. It slips and wavers, as though it finds folds, varying densities in its path, obstacle, a magnetic resistance invisible, not daunting. The pools suck down blackness, and I'm with the dragonflies. I smell orange-blossom, my bank is heavy with it, and over there – weak brown sheep, little bigger than cats: the water runs too fast for their thin tongues. Here – I lie on hyacinths, the stems squeak like wicker: their life is cold, the horses push through these flowers, creaking, as if they're wearing new boots. And the dragonflies: flick, flick. One held, and holding: the other struggling up the current, a gymnast; the first patterns, intuitions, run through ...

LENIN IN THE CINEMA

'For us, the cinema is the most important of the arts.'

V.I. Lenin

ANOTHER DAY at work. The drawing office. Wet Paris mornings, where everyone looks like someone else: someone important, someone alive or dead. I set up my work, use it to conceal my pleasure, my cartoon. Paris was the capital of revolutions, then of the cinema: then, for a little while that is perhaps not over, of the cartoon. Will a Lenin find the cartoon a revolutionary art? And rescue me? Set me up there with the big names, the recognisable faces – make history of me? I start my story: 'The lion of the Amazon' – too enigmatic. 'The treasure of Xica da Silva' – the slave who made a fortune. Or shall I identify too much? And yet, for the Amazon, we need a queen, an Amazonian, Brazilian knockout, like young Xica.

'Millions of heads, like black peppercorns, or matchsticks with dobs of red, of white, phosphorous. Bands with American tubas – their heads swaying like pythons'. Security men in Ray-Bans, feeling suspect bulges among the crowd: "Hey, man, what you carrying here, a Magnum?"

'"Hey, right man, you right. That's what I carrying."

'Gathered here in the name of the ballot and. the unity of the species, on the banks of this 32-lane freeway, inaugurating the first lady president of the hemisphere, an enthusiastic lesbian, not yet 24. Photo xeroxed, pasted on thousand-dollar bills and scattered to the crowds.

'What enthusiasm! Here a guy selling cans of Bud, knocked down and trampled. There a small landslip slides a samba group down and out, into the headlines. Union of Brazil and Argentina, Brazentina: continental euphoria.

'She sits up there, surrounded by her Amazons, all newly promoted general, and every one a samba queen. All ready for the hunt, beautiful black and white skins setting off the golden braid, little bows and arrows stolen from the Indians – a double row of cheesecake cupids. All ready for the hunt, across the sierra, across the pampas, into the rain forests, ready for the hunt... '

I can't focus, the picture fades. Xica da Silva came here, in her short real life, came to Paris. After her, but not because of her, the revolution. The director of my first, real job comes in. He has a famous face, an unenviable one. You say at once: 'Aldo Moro'. Aldo Moro has been a cadaver for ten years, but already he is looking better. He was – he is – a true saint in sheep's clothing, but as clever as he's devout. Eating his madeleine, he looks like Mrs Sheep in her shop. Being dead doesn't mean too much to him – no doubt he thinks that this is heaven. Ever-pressing fear of hell, already he has his sinners and his devils courting him. He'll put in a word for them, they think, and rip them off a touch as well: himself he did not save. I slide away, from hierarchies here, and I'm back, back on the drawing board, back in Brazil.

'The lady president abolishes sex and dissent for the duration of the hunt. Electronically, the votes against her are transformed into positive ones. She and all her company take a vow of chastity. All other world leaders follow suit – except the pope, who institutes a regime of non-stop orgies. To prepare herself spiritually, the queen-slave-president goes down to hell. It looks like Milwaukee. She is a beautiful glass flower.'

I break away from my narcissism, and watch the director in his office. Moro is praying again. The phone rings. He speaks to it. He hangs up, but continues conversing. I see he has the porter, a baggy Gorbachev, in a corner of the room. He is berating Gorbachev for bullying behaviour in the elevator. He says there have been complaints, and Gorbachev is sweating, accusing his enemies among the neighbours. Moro is unyielding, but in the end, with his little smile, he yields. Gorbachev barges his way down the corridor, and pushes his way into the lift. He ignores poor Ronnie Reagan, who is collecting our bets on the evening's cycle racing. And Moro calls Ronnie into his office. Mildly, he reproves him for a wasted old age. Ronnie will start to cry.

I can't stand this bathos, force myself back to my story:

'The President, Candida, is challenged by tourists from the future. They are living in the *barrios*, the *favelas*, they want to change the course of time, turn Candida's successes into failures. Why? They must be bored. They wear masks because human faces have become so ugly. They run everywhere, like Inca messengers. The world has no more fuel. On weekends you can skateboard.'

I can't go on. I must be bored. I must have a beer, meet with my new friends, Lenin and Trotsky. Is it possible they hardly know each other? I slide out of the building, and see Moro's long face at the window. He is the cow, and I'm the cowslip. Gorbachev is playing cards on a box in the street. He is slamming down his cards, 'and one: and two: and the clincher'. He is playing with César Auguste, the big black who always beats him, and cheats. César Auguste tells me he is 35, but his hair is white: he looks like a pot-scourer.

Lenin is prematurely bald. Prematurely for what, I don't know. He is always in this bar, playing tric-trac, or, as now, vigorously annotating *Of Grammatology*, a book he says is tops but I suspect he doesn't understand. I usually see him here with Trotsky. They are regulars here, but they only speak to each other when I'm around. Sometimes Lenin tries to talk to the Algerians, needling them, till they tell him to piss off. 'Piss off, piss off,' he repeats. 'Yes, you've learned the language of reason all right.'

I ask him, 'Where's Trotsky?' I never talk about my cartoons, the revolution he, or the Amazonian queen, should lead: but he knows all about my job, the office, Moro, Gorbachev.

He answers, 'Trotsky's doing his martial arts, I believe. He insists his puny physique's an advantage.'

Lenin himself is no Hercules, and his skin is yellow and wrinkled like a pickled brain. I can't think what to say. 'I hear Trotsky is being rehabilitated over there.'

Lenin is suddenly animated. 'What a disgrace! I'd sooner rot than have that happen! Talk about skinning the ox twice!'

I am stuck in this bar, stuck in this city, with a deflated Lenin who won't play his part. A little effort, and I'm in Brazentina once again. 'Candida cannot find the way out of her city. The city has excluded the colours red and green. This means the traffic lights in every district have different phases – from violet through turquoise to brown, from orange to blue to diamond white. But her city stretches for ever, like an immense production line, or gut – showrooms to wreckers' yards, courts and hospitals, each zone packed with people of a different colour.'

I wait for Trotsky.

Lenin says, 'Trotsky's always late.' He's in a nervous mood. He often rants on about the others. He calls

Gorbachev 'Motormouth', but I think he may be jealous. Of me? I don't know why. I've taken the same oath as Candida. It has become hard to enjoy glory or death in the first person. Some larger figure seems to intervene, to find the right words, of regret, of condemnation. I feel I shall not even be sorry for myself, someone more powerful, skilled, or just more sensitive, will do it for me. Even Lenin is better informed about my fantasies than I, although he's unemployed, and Trotsky has problems with the rent. Trotsky doesn't look as much like Trotsky, though, as Lenin looks like Lenin.

I ask Lenin: 'Are there lions in the rain forests?' and he replies, 'In the rain forests there is everything.'

In my head I draw the pictures of the words: it is indeed the Amazonian lion that Candida hopes to find. That is indeed her programme. That she was elected on. The lion: described by the many writers of the zone – for this is the real treasure of Xica da Silva – apart from its long legs and musky smell, its features are: its orange teeth, and a mane that passes through three phases – from black beneath, to blue, and then smoke-grey. Its tail-end is held high, the tuft is black enamel, a kind of policeman's badge, or maybe a cockade. It's hard to see, to concentrate on, because you are held by those pale eyes, like grape-flesh, in the dusk they go to quince, the pupils inflexible, like two typed 'l's. And when it speaks...

Trotsky parks his motorbike, and comes in with his messenger's satchel. I don't trust him. Things I say only to him and Lenin seem to get back to Moro. Moro has spoken to me about lions. I've seen Moro and Trotsky together in another bar, eating steamed potatoes and salt herring. I know that Trotsky bets, and wins, with Ronnie Reagan, but he never treats us. Lenin and I owe so much money in this bar, it would take some huge upset to set us free –

meanwhile, we are obliged to keep on coming. Trotsky is lucky to have a messenger's job: it's good news, if you bet. There's no future in it. But future for what?

I am back in the land of the lion, the forest: 'None of the freeways leaves Candida's city. They circle it like the grooves on a record. Some of her escort are hurt in road accidents. They are seized and used for spare parts by gangs holed up in hospitals, experimenting with immortality.'

Trotsky says, 'I can't wait till the last real Parisian leaves. It'll be better when there's only exiles here.'

Lenin is irritated. 'Not exiles, immigrants.'

Trotsky replies, 'Well, I prefer being an exile – it's not a question of nationality.'

I know they've always lived here. Trotsky drinks my beer and rushes out. 'This district's going downhill fast,' he says. 'All kinds of funny business.' He looks like a philosophy prof, and Lenin his mature pupil who can never graduate.

Lenin says, 'I'd like to ask you out. But I don't have any money. Perhaps you'd like to ask me out?'

I say, 'Well, anyway, where would we go?'

We pause outside my building. I must go in, pretend to be working. Lenin's going to the cinema. Reagan is protesting about something. Usually he's quiet. Lenin says, 'They're arresting Ronnie. Gambling. Serve him right.'

Gorbachev is busy with a broom, sweeping out the courtyard. There seems a great quantity of leaves, but I had never seen a tree there. He makes no move to intervene in Ronnie's plight.

Lenin dismisses the incident. 'Of all the arts, the cartoon is, for the moment, the most important. But – those little boxes the pictures are in, and those little bags for the words!'

I say abstractedly, 'You can do anything you like – it's like the blues, it's like opera, without music, but you could make videos and add everything ... It's like drawing the inside of your head.'

I think, 'Perhaps Moro will sort out Ronnie's problem,' but then I wonder if he hasn't sent for the cops himself. I must concentrate on my own story:

'Candida finds the rain forests only a few metres from the ramparts of the city. Her comrades must board a tall ruined galleon, manned by black admirals. They go down through galleries and passageways lined with stone animals, their pupils fixed and inflexible, like typed '1's. In the city, the travellers from the future are speeding up the seasons. Winter lasts only a few days, in a few minutes spring has come, the fruit and flowers burst out like roman candles. The people are enthralled – but they are ageing, slowing down; as they gape, their teeth fall out, their limbs wither ... The city falls to ruin, the rivers are red with rust.'

I see Gorbachev taking sacks of leaves from César Auguste, and sending him away for more. He empties them out, and sweeps them up again.

I must get to the lion: 'In the hold of the galleon, they find the lion. He is lying on a white vinyl couch, and around him are the lights and reflectors for television. Candida has only three of her most faithful lovers to accompany her. The admirals crowd round, their wiry white hair looks like pot-scourers.'

Lenin hisses to me, 'It's that bugger Trotsky', and then leaps forward, like a balding jackal, pushes the cop and sends him sprawling as he's ushering Ronnie Reagan away. The cop can't see what's happening, and Lenin is really very quick, very practised. He shouts to Ronnie, who is struck still like some stone animal, 'Run, you twerp', and slowly Ronnie scutters off.

The cop gets up and runs to the metro after Lenin. But I see that Lenin is over there, talking to the girl on the cinema box-office. They seem good pals. So that's how he sees so many films. Gorbachev is leaning expressionless on his broom: the courtyard is clear, but I can see a space by the wall now filled with neatly stacked bags of leaves. César Auguste has disappeared.

I am at my desk. I must finish the cartoon. I feel like the pilot of a black bomber flying over a silver sea, the radio antenna is like cobwebs. I am hurrying, I am rushing the story of Candida, I have been trite about Xica da Silva. My lion is not the Brazilian revolution, nor yet an ecowizard.

'The lion is old and chilled. He doesn't eat gazelles, but drinks carrot-juice and pops testerone pills. He now puts on Ray-Bans and a shawl embroidered with strawberry leaves. Candida has become old and fat after her adventures, and with her three attendants she looks like a malign pumpkin surrounded by witches. She asks the lion the three questions: first, to test him – since we see the answer on a screen behind him, "How shall I die?" and he tells her.

'Secondly, "Shall I fulfil my mandate, and be successful?"

'The lion chuckles: "What do you think?"

'Finally, she asks, "Is it worth it?"

'The lion closes his magnificent eyes, which have become a diamond-white under the lights, the pupils, like two typed "l"s, as narrow as keyholes. He is asleep.

'But these answers restore Candida. She longs to be away, and regain her city in a last battle. The admirals form up behind her and her court, making a clangourous *afoxé* behind her Zis convertible, drawn by mules – a crepitating, shuffling swarm, 158 abreast, back along the Avenue of the Americas, swinging round Radio Square and into Silicon Alley.'

Moro calls me. He had been watching everything from above. I thought I saw his sheep's head peeking from behind the blinds. I feel that cartoon days are nearly done. He has seen me, with Lenin. 'I'm afraid,' he says, showing his long, orange teeth, 'I shall have to let you go, Chantal. Not that I ever *really* let anyone *go*, my dear girl (and what a lovely name yours is), but – now there is a closeness, now a distance. Now you'll do your drawings on your time, not on mine.' He chuckles, and his pupils constrict into two typed '1's.

I can see, far below, Gorbachev handing the broom to Reagan, who looks dumbstruck, like a garden gnome. The last of the bags of leaves is disappearing to the roadway, César Auguste is toting it. In their own ways, Lenin and Trotsky have let me down.

I am through. The story finishes: 'Candida must fight her last battle alone, regain her city from the time travellers. She fills the subway, transforming herself into a hydra, as a hatch of mayfly she aerates the rivers, and as a fall of steel feathers – amber, lilac, black – she cleanses the air. Time slows down again, the seasons drag out. People age, but slowly. Terribly slowly. Life becomes imperceptible again, in its passing. Candida looks younger and younger.

'She has triumphed, again she is surrounded by bright lovers. We are back on the banks of the 32-lane freeway. Millions of heads, like black peppercorns, or matchsticks with dobs of red, of white, phosphorous …'

I am liberated, whether I want it or not, freer than Candida, freer even than Xica da Silva. Lenin has lived up to the name I've given him

.

GENIUS

Genius is the ability to survive impossible situations.
Jean-Paul Sartre

THE GRANDSON peers down the stair-well. Smooth marble, perhaps some synthetic stone, its secret now forgotten. He sees, far below, in the light greenish, dusty sun, his grandfather. His grandfather is animated, on his bald head there is perhaps a fly, perhaps just a vein flickers to give the excuse for broad gestures, intimations of an itch. The grandson thinks of those jokey pictures, where the marbled skull has a fly on it, the public drawn from veneration to brush it away – their gesture the reason for the being of the guardian in uniform seated in the corner. His life's work to arrest that public gesture, prevent the painted fly being knocked off the painted skull.

His grandfather bends over a deep deep well, like the stairs held in an art deco ellipse, the water a cold green, and there, far at the bottom, a white fish, a white flesh, a naked woman, taking some special underwater cure for fatness. Between the grandfather and the grandson a head, somewhere at the middle of the stair, pokes out like an iron muzzle: his father's head, his son's head. The grandfather, in this memory, is deeply into fascism. Probably the Duce is outside somewhere in hot boots, cursing the organisers of some parade, the sun, his fury puffing him up: dreaming of piles of skulls, never enough. The grandfather is doing well: he has a marble staircase, and a marble bath for quackery. The father – his son – will be an honest man, but less successful, and his son, the grandson, now at the top of the tree, the stairs, a little less successful, and so less honest, than the pair of them.

All three of them are geniuses. The grandfather is trying to sell genius, it being fascism and the times are hard; the son will try to give his away, it being the turn of communism, and sacrifice all round; and it's the grandson who will try to go against nature, do something that will really challenge all the family trees and stairs: something fascism and communism in their wholly different ways – grandfather a conman and exploiter, the son – the father – a victim-philanthropist – wouldn't have considered even right, or even necessary. For genius is often metaphorised into marble, into diamonds, but it's also quite like treacle, or like tar, sticky, sweet, or even quite repellent to the taste.

*

'Genius,' said the grandfather, 'Gives us a poor time with women, a distant time. And they – the authorities – felt genius was a fascist thing. Well, not democratic, certainly.' He pauses: should he go further? 'Mussolini wanted me to get rid of his fat. But he wouldn't sink, and he couldn't hold his breath. The idea is that depth, the cold of the water, the aversion to drowning – all that would burn it off: and then my prices – they made you think before going for another blowout! But Mussolini couldn't handle it.'

'But, father,' the son – the father – asks the grandfather, 'you were in with them, the bosses, the gerarchs, the rasses?'

'I got our money from them, certainly. Never from the poor, you can't anyway get money from the poor, nor yet the skinny,' and he laughs a high cracked note like the Angelus bell, 'I never sank to exploiting the poor, though that too will come. When we are equal, Stanislaus, when the poor exploit the poor, then we shall have democracy. And then, on tiptoe, I shall raise my hat. "Goodnight, good gentlemen, it's late for me, goodnight, I do not think that this last game's for me."'

'Father, you never wear a hat,' says the son, the father, affectionately.

The old man has seen many massacres. Officially, as an official, and then, much later, when you start to think only of your own death, the cart you drag that ends up heavier and heavier, finally it overtakes the horse – yourself – more massacres. The winters massacring: the peasants drinking antifreeze, the trains running on time unpublished but precise, carrying the passengers here to massacre, and there – to massacre.

The grandfather says, 'What could a genius do then? A super-massacre to end it all. A soft gun with a myriad barrels to shoot us all stone dead as we slept, a super-frost to kill us like dogs pointing as we guarded in the night. Nothing, however, in nature ever repeats itself, and that is why we know there are emotions. They get in through the gaps, and they are why we kill, are killed. Perhaps why we die.' He coughs in apology. 'But at least, I held firm. I resisted.'

His son says, 'But without courage.'

'Without courage, yes. But with great persistence. A great honesty in persistence.'

He pauses. 'I was always in positions to grasp the generosity of others – I was the witness of their courage.' Another, massacring, pause: 'For what it was worth,' and quickly adds, 'Worth to me, I mean, not them, of course.'

*

The grandfather has projects, the father, impressions; the
son, a design. The grandfather called his son Stanislaus, not
because of the winter campaign in the USSR, not because of
any political turns of tides, but for Joyce's brother, another
angle on genius, a genius at an angle to a genius.
Grandfather pulls back lips, almost the colour of liver, and
says, 'The pity, that our species is so – carnivorous,' and
grins with his two teeth sticking out, a Dracula, a lone wolf,
as if to show that of the real, the fearsome horrors, there
aren't that many left, already howling towards extinction.
He says to his son, Stanislaus, 'Of all the massacres, the
worst I saw was in that village, the Americans thought it
was quite another, quite a different village, of quite a
different importance, but the villagers knew quite well
where they were, and the bombs came down by accident, it
was like a miracle, with the walls all going down, the arms
and legs, alas, all going up and down, and only we deserters,
and the mules and donkeys, in stout rocky cellars, safe. And
it was then my project changed. I thought – not fat, not the
deep baths, but gas: that is the answer. Intestinal gas – the
motive and emotive power. The key to passions, and the
means for traction. Attraction – traction.'

    'You mean,' says Stanislaus, ready to get a laugh for, out
of, his grandfather, 'Mussolini's pulling-power lay in his
farts?'

    'Exactly, dear boy. Farting in public. That's why we
couldn't get him down to the bottom of our pool. But think
– those guts linked to pistons, propellers, a Hindenberg of
immense capacity.'

But Stanislaus is not enthused, he's heard this claptrap all before. Genius would be to get Mussolini fitted up as a combustion device.

His grandfather says, 'That village, I recall, had trouble with the French troops, the revolutionaries – requisitioning mules for harvest, the villagers hid them, and the village was burned down,' and he cackles like a pile of halms burning, and Stanislaus carefully sets the problem along some Party line, judiciously sets his own and keeps it to himself, certainly none of the parties, mules, villagers, Napoleon's men, Stanislaus, the Party – are better off, but then, dialectics is not a soup kitchen but a wonderful marriage of kaleidoscope and telescope.

Stanislaus is interested in his impressions, not the grandfather's projects – his father's projects. He trudges round Europe, finding impressions – they may be a woodcut, a clumsy old diamond, a confessional, a dog-cart, some rusty clothes, a copy of some picture that looks familiar. And these he sells, or fails to sell, living on his wits, his genius, 'And all the time on Party business?' asks his son, 'Not always,' the reply, meaning hardly ever, what would the Party want from this kind of essence, of completeness, redolence, the quiddity?

He tells his son, 'A true collector chooses just the single piece, passing over all the others,' but in this case Stanislaus is not a real collector, for he brings back all kind of immemorabilia, mounted moths moth-eaten, glass bowls for hanging goldfish in, complete sets of hotel room keys, maps of subway systems. In his own brilliant mind, ideologies have already dissolved, everywhere has moved on and over from itself, the parties have all ceased activity and changed their names, the rousing regimes have packed away their drums and trumpets, and the great nursery plan – the tree house, the eternal summer holiday, the neighbourhood gang, the peeking (or gawping) at the rich kids – all these extravagant schemes come to an end and school begins again, tougher lessons though, and Stanislaus is saved from disillusion not by genius but by some quiet old-fashioned taste. So that some of his findings – the mirror from Burgos opalescent like grease, the *naif* crucifixion from Peć with the crescent-shaped nails – someone will buy them. Someone will buy these keepsakes, pay a tribute to the wandering Stanislaus, who gradually comes to learn everything about everything, so when the Party founders under him, he scarcely notices. It has become a wife, embarrassing with all her flirts and picayune habits, and Stanislaus ponders over her gravestone: does he 'sadly' miss her, 'deeply' miss her, or is his decision never to re-marry comment enough on the old harridan, even, he thinks, the old harlot?

The question anyway is one for genius, since Stanislaus's family was acquired sidestepping marriage, in the least painful way. *His* son the product, maybe, of a warning against death, maybe of death itself. The son a kind of legacy, of the figure in a coffin that might have been an unknown father-in-law, and for his son a grandfather. Or just some unknown; death himself; his wife's lover, perhaps even the father of this son, and so, in a kind of tidy way, his brother?

And that sorts out his son, kind of, and death and birth, but not the mother of his son (a fascist? Spanish? Mad? A mad Spanish fascist?) – and not his wife, the Party-metaphor.

He thinks of Leibniz and is glad he never knew how, when or why his own, his only, father died. Which means, of course, that probably the old man didn't go, will never go, but just sank down and out of sight, like those fish in Lake Baikal that fight the instinct to come up to the light (or maybe never even see it, have no 'up' that's light or dark) – and if they do, explode: bodies, the atmosphere detonating them, and immediately resolving the problem of their fat, or if they were Mussolini, extinguishing themselves in total fart.

*

'I was in Spain,' said the father. 'In the church, under the lamps a set of flies was whirling. Exploring the corners of a barn dance: a computer working out equations. A child playing cat's cradle. You know flies, you've seen them?' he asks the child, the son, who nods.

'Then I saw, beneath the flies, the coffin. A face like a great cheese but two eyebrows darkly drawing together like two meat hooks, a nose like an owl's beak, and lips like two pale threads of liver. And dead, quite quite dead.'

The father mimes being nailed to the spot. 'And then I see a woman in black, but not lace, just like black jeans, oilcloth. It is your mother. She leads me into a robing room. I remember the body – he held a miniature, like Spanish court portraits of the sixteenth century, and she was the grown version of the miniature. Her father, dead? Grandfather? Brother? She pulls me into these white and purple vestments, the arsenic green, that ecclesiastical violet: it was terribly hot, or you'd think it was spring, entering so many crocuses, or maybe folds of the body, but bodies deteriorating, meat rotting. And so hot. And then a priest comes in, he strips naked quite naked, but not as you'd expect, a young body, but an old one, the hair rubbed off the buttocks like an old fur rug, veins popping out everywhere. And as he prepares to robe, he farts, and under cover of that, we depart. But an awful fart, like viscera in a jar unstoppered after months. Then she draws me through a dining room, that smell of rancid oil, a basket full of bottles: McGinnis OLD Kentucky Katsup. Then a laundry room, and then a huge depository for priests' umbrellas, all broken, there must have been acolytes or penitents whose lives were spent repairing them? What with? Other umbrellas?'

Reluctantly, the father goes on. 'And so, pulling me here and there, I finally came to realise, though at different times, and with different modalities, that this was to be, and now, time being what it is, that this had been, your mother. And that these rooms – the bar across the street, the game of billiards – well, it struck me before we were out of the church and its outworks. The chambers of the pyramid. From the centre to the outside. From the mystery of the burial chamber to the false tomb, to the treasure, the slaves, the banqueting hall.'

The son asks, 'But her purpose was quite different? Not to save you from entombment, from burial with the – whoever. The great chief. The big cheese-face.'

'Quite, quite different. And when we had made love – or, rather, when I had made love and she had made love, or better, when I had entered upon the mystery, and when she had revealed, I think, quite another one.' He pauses, and the son is impatient. The father goes on, 'She asked me to put out the garbage. In the alley, masses of garbage she had, cigar butts and ashes, decks of cards, .22 long cartridges – only the boxes, of course. "It was time to put out the garbage," she said. And by God she was right.'

The son thinks of pyramids and the coppery desert outside, strewn with long .22 cartridge cases, bandits with cues strapped to their saddles like bow cases, their heads wrapped in embalming cloths against the dust.

The father says, 'And only later did I see, the black, the grey the yellow in the church, the arsenic green of that mint drink at the bar. The tantra! We went through all the colours of the tantra, and only later did I see that! She was not a saviour and a messenger, but, in her way, a seer.'

The son asks, 'But you didn't believe all that?'

'Naturally not. If there was anything to believe or disbelieve: I just recognised the colours, the pink of the gecko, wrongly called a salamander, the bowels of the dead ruler drawn through the skull as if the brain and the intestine were the same corruptible organ. I recognised it all, of course.'

The son prompts, 'And then, suddenly, there I was.'

'Yes, ten years later, there you were. Delivered by train.'

The son asks, in love with his own story, 'How did you know it was me?'

The question puzzles the father. 'That you were your mother's son? That you were conceived on that busy afternoon? That I owed you bed and board? Well, a little man of ten gets over lots of the troubles of fatherhood. But of course, I don't chop logic. It would be odd if the questions all turned out to have the same answer. No, what I recognised in you was genius. And, of course, you were addressed.'

They contemplate the infinite chain of coincidence which places them together face to face in this room at this time.

The son says, 'I had a football.'

The father says, 'You had had a football. A major had thrown it off the train.'

The son says, 'But not a mystery. Though an odd toy to take on a train journey, from Spain to France. But you were still a comrade? You think it might have been full of plans, information? Landing in a field near Leon. Ball in the face waking the officer, infuriating him?'

The father says, 'Yes, I was a comrade, that's why in part I went to Franco's Spain.'

The son knows his story thoroughly. 'If I knew it was a major, you can be sure I knew the football was empty: no cash, no plans.'

The father assents, wistfully. 'But you might have the rank wrong. He might have been deserting. The panels in the football stitched in a certain way? The leather even, sometimes gave a clue. Though, I admit, only that genius was communicating unto genius, haha,' he laughs, but is not convinced, is not convinced that anything at all funny has been said.

*

The son is very drunk. He can't remember what he's drinking. He is in a Chinese restaurant, a long, serpentine boiler room, shaped and decorated like the bed of the Tiber, fish boiled and fried, offered from stalls, receptacles in the walls, the banks – sea worms, grey cod, grey carp, grey dragons. It is very hot: the son says, 'My grandfather was Claudio Tagliacozzo,' which is a lie. He says, 'My father was Arcangelo Piras', and this was a lie too, no one in his family is known to be Jewish, nor a Sard, he himself speaks with a heavy Spanish accent when he's drunk.

A Chinese says, 'This lady has been separated from her party', and they walk down the river bed, eating together. The fish are kept in grass, in the cubbyholes, as if they are resting in a catacomb. It is terribly hot. The son tells her his name: 'I'm Eugenio,' and he is very drunk, but doesn't feel drunk. They rub their bodies together. She seems to like this. Her back is bare, and they rub themselves on every piece of bare flesh. It is as if they are eating one another. It is as if they have eaten one another. She rubs her breasts against him.

Eugenio knows he cannot have seen his grandfather at the bottom of the stair-well, he doubts he can ever have seen his father and his grandfather together. Both of them just petered out. Perhaps they are alive. The men in the kitchens are arguing and bringing down cleavers as points of emphasis, thwack, *cling*, and hawking and cursing. Eugenio says to the woman, separated from her party, 'My father went many times to China. He was a brilliant man. He worked for the communists, but in the end he felt they were too human. I think he would have preferred ...' he wants to say his father would have preferred it if they had been less Chinese, but this is an unpardonable thing to say. The woman takes his hands and they rub against each other, back to back.

He lets the manager take the money for all the fish they have eaten, and he's so drunk he is glad that he'll find out what it cost only tomorrow. The woman says, 'And you could give me eighty dollars. Or a hundred and twenty,' and he hands her his wallet.

Later, they make love, with great difficulty (he is very drunk), but to him it does not seem a paid service, though he can't say why. Perhaps because he is so drunk, it all takes a long time, and from many angles, and much detail. So, he thinks of an act of love, or at least of many, unclear emotions. As she leaves him, he says clumsily, 'I hope you find your party,' and she reacts to this joke, or courtesy, by making an angry face. He wonders sometimes if a ten-year-old will arrive one day, an address label round their wrist, speaking Italianate Chinese and wearing some young version of his face, or hers.

*

Eugenio said, 'Of course, you can have rights without knowing it, without understanding them.'

'Of course,' agrees the foundress, 'But if the creatures understood, even a little, we would be so much more convincing as their champions.'

So Eugenio, half with a wink, half with a sigh, half with a brush of his sleeve against the dust on his Leibniz, half with relief that his pay no longer depended directly on the whims of human beings, went to work as philosopher for the animals in the Foundation for Rights-in-general. He dissociated himself from working for people. 'It doesn't seem apposite, given my antecedents,' he says, though not knowing with any precision what these are.

He does not, of course, teach philosophy to the rats – who are eager to learn but have the wrong kind of brain surface: the cats, who are quick but impenetrably sceptical, and the dogs, omnivorous for information but unable to recognise connections. Instead, he creates a caring environment; he manufactures, observes and grades rights-laden situations. He has, of course, his own secret project which involves non-carnivores. He has much light-hearted trust in earthworms, as legitimate heirs of everything we leave, including anything digestible from our ethics.

He does not go very far. He stereotypes the animal species. After the incident in the Yellow River Restaurant, he has taken to stereotyping human situations. All those fishes, some reduced to skeletons, vomited up, still articulated, the next morning.

*

Eugenio sees a newspaper obituary of his grandfather, and thinks of the *spack* of fish exploding in the tank as demonstrations of the power of deep water therapy. But there is nothing of that, and it seems it's a mistake, partial, total, and his father's life is being told, 'remarkable mediation with the Spanish communists to accept the successors to the Regime ... crowning accomplishment ... the dissolution of his own party, in an age now less ideological than divided by questions of material substance,' and Eugenio grins, thinking of the tantra. 'Always a democratic liberal rather than a liberal democrat', the paper buzzes on unaware the subject too is guffawing at the terms, 'at heart', the description; 'a man of the left but not of extremes'.

Eugenio waits for his father's letter which will put all their lives and deaths in perspective. It is hermetic, but asks for money, 'a tempting business project for your spare cash, or savings', refers to 'the Spanish lady, your mother, now translated into a "*socialist*" I hear' – how?

Then there is a fierce attack on Eugenio's work, 'Breaking down the last defence that keeps, protects, one species from another ... insane impulse to communicate at all costs that ill-conceals the human will to dominate by juridical orders ... leave the poor cats and fish alone, to fight it out, if that is how you see it ... none of us carnivores has long on earth,' and suggesting that the flies over the coffin in Leon – had it been Leon? – were a living digital computer telling off the ages of man.

'All we have, Eugenio,' the letter ends, 'is our genius: at worst our wits, at best our capacity to map the tide of history, and then to find our patch of dry. The river bed after the flood, the Chinese say, is safer than the highest treetop.'

But then too, Eugenio thinks as he goes to the airport to collect a shipment of earthworms, a kind that is able to digest papyrus and is said to construct vast underground warrens – floods don't just happen, they are caused as part of cycles, of land speculation, of irrigation, of human neglect and need.

He goes to the customs shed, and as he usually does, he wonders if he will go away with a cage of intelligent worms or a ten-year-old daughter, an airline label on her wrist, who will tell him of her life in Macao and, when the evenings lengthen, of the travels of Fa Hsien in India.

And then he will know everything about everything, just like his father.

As he waits, he thinks of telling her about his conception, and about hers, and of a story that his father might have told him, about the fat, happy communists once, when the water was deep and black and clean, letting down their lights into Lake Baikal, bringing the pressurised fish up, up towards the surface, until suffused with that brilliant golden light the fish burst, with joy, under a brilliant starlit sky.

THE NORTHLAND

I T'S DAWN, a long time ago. Off the Greyhound, looking for work. Difficult to find work that's not hard. Hard to find work that's not difficult.

Past the prison farm, its protective hedges of black stinging flies, bigger than in Siberia. Better food here. More prisoners.

Look at the multicoloured waters. Brown water, green water, black, yellow, grey. Blue water looks anomalous. Tailings, ponds look ashamed. Rocks browned and burnt black. Thin birches, smell of new rubber. Little trains up on the crest: tipping down fire, dragons' tails just slag down grey, burnt out ash.

Don't want to go down the fucking mine; only thing they've got here. Give the earth a rest, leave its guts alone. Nickel for bullets and for plating tanks. Battle for the earth still undecided. Aliens needed for the decisive battle. Down the hole. Hell, no. I won't go.

Off the bus with Roman, my new friend. He's coming home, off our pilgrimage, the northern route, Wawa to Rouyn. Perhaps to drive the ore trains. He asks, 'Why you go to a mining town if you don't want to go down the fucking mine?'

He doesn't like the mine at all, but worked them all, from out east, from coal to cobalt, then gold is hot, 'Then you go down in asbestos, gives you something else, but no so hot'.

Talks like a Frenchman, but doesn't say too much. Takes me to this old guy, an old, old Finn, his face is silver like a birch, his clothes all black and black felt, like stuff out the roof. Mr Vapaus, and he says to me, 'You an Indian', and I say, 'No, just kind of shabby, stepping out of nature in this way,' and he asks, 'Your hat,' 'Yes,' I tell him, 'Yes, an Indian gave me.' It was a Micmac, and he told me another Indian gave it him, and so it passes along the northland's path of guys like me, who have to look for work, and don't much like it when they have it, especially if it's down the fucking mine.

Mr Vapaus says, 'You Indians higher than a Frenchman, but should be back in nature, all of you,' and I only think to say, 'It's boring for them Indians, just with the same bunch of people that you know, and maybe selling blueberries,' but Roman is telling him, 'Mr Vapaus, now, we want to work, but not go down that mine, nor even in that smelter,' and the Finn has heard it all before.

He says, 'You go down that mine, there's everything. There's Frenchmen, Indians, communists, there's Russians red and white, there's Finns, Ukrainians white and red, and most of all there's guys who didn't want to go,' and there is smoke all round, everything is blowing, blowing smoke – the little ore trains on the crest, and the high stacks, and a group of guys with long Cuban cigarettes.

We spend the day not going down the mine. Drinking tequila in a lounge, and Roman says the good kind has a worm in and when you get to it, that tastes like tequila too, and perhaps the worm thinks as it eats you, you taste of tequila too.

A trapper brings in a big beaver, with an evil eye, its tail slaps against each table, and I make the sign against its eye, but Roman says, 'Well, you'd look angry too, if you was dying,' and he ought to know, because the girl who had his little girl went with a miner who went poking at a chimney that was plugged, down there, and got a thirty ton of rock down on his head; and that's why Roman doesn't say so much, even though he's younger than me by quite a bit, he's had all his experiences now, just chews them over, quietly, not letting you see if there's smoke or fire.

And so we have that bottle, and another one, and at how many bucks a shot – the mine is getting nearer, and the smoke goes shooting up, the guys come off one shift, go on another, and a guy tells us if we draw the smelter, not to go on the dust machine.

'All you do is watch it. Watch the dial. And if it goes too high, then what your job is, is run like hell. It sends you crazy, all the time, just watch the dial, watch the dial.'

And Roman asks him if, all things considered, the life's hard there. 'No, no. There isn't anything to do. The union takes care of that, if you're unskilled. Just stand where no one can see you. But you must show up for work. And mind if they blow your section, boy, or your head comes out that mine quicker'n your body,' and I think it will be better for us all, when we aren't here any more at all, all the troublemakers kicked out somewhere.

'But where'll we all go?' I ask, and Roman says, 'They'll find some other hole to put us all, some other hole, some other ground,' but it still seems to me life would be more integrated if we had some other place to go.

We listen to some other guys, some union guys, and they are saying when the company tries to bring another union in, and how someone was caught, shooting at the helicopters, the mounties flying them, and got off by saying the rifle was a toy, 'Yeah, and the little helicopters up so high, with toy pigs riding in them,' and in between all this, I win a girl at shuffleboard. I win her off the guy she's with. One thing I did improve, I'd say perfected, was shooting that straight-board, after I'd quit school, and not from being stupid, just not having much to say and getting it down straight – the summer before I banged up that long line of cars through driving on too straight, and too precise, and being stubborn.

She was a good shooter too, and French, and even better on the board than me, especially now that things were getting drunker. Her name, 'Madeleine', she kept saying and I forgetting, and she again, 'Mad'len, you duff head, what are you, some stupid Indian?' and I'd just laugh, and say, 'Just my hat – an Indian gave,' until she laughed and said I wasn't clever enough to be French, but at least I wasn't a fucking anglo, and I said her face looked like a doll's, not because hers specially did, but because at that point almost everyone looked either a beaver or a doll. And she says, 'I do things a doll can't,' and I say, 'You do things a doll won't', and that made her fasten on to Roman for a while, who just stays quiet, quiet, and then she says, 'I'm making up to him to divert suspicions,' but of what I couldn't think. She liked being in the middle, she said, between two pigs, but she wasn't lesbian, and we won a heap of money at the shuffleboard, and drank ourselves right through the other side, to a sobriety and peace, as if the mine closed down, there was a strike, the water turned all blue, and all us guys – well, what? Just disappeared. Turned into hermits.

Madeleine took us out, and drove us round a bit, and says to Roman he should look after me, at least better than he does, and then he showed the pictures of his family and the little girl, and that put Mad'len back with me, and Roman felt cut out, and he insisted, he forced us, to go to Mr Vapaus. And I knew the scheme was terrible, but Roman was determined, and Mad'len went all soft, and says she likes to be accomplice, and so my body drifts along, into the mess, my mind just stays outside and hums, like it's not interested, but knows a heap of other, more absorbing things. And it did seem the way of stop going down the mine, stop being suckered down into that black hole.

Roman said that all the Finns had guns, if was for the revolution, or if not, then for bears, and maybe other Finns. And Mr Vapaus let us have the gun, although he said he'd only lend it if we didn't load it. And Madeleine said we were all drunk or crazy, and no fun and dangerous. And if we didn't get ourselves killed, or caught, she'd drive us out of town next day, and fix a place, but now her fucking shift was starting, and I suspect she meant her old man had just got off his, and so she should go home – but the suspicion came slowly, over many years, and at the time all I felt was betrayed.

And it seems that if you don't go down the fucking mine, you end up as a deviant with a gun, though mostly you aren't so lucky as to find someone will lend you one so easy. And Roman boasted that he knew the manager at the Motor Inn, and if we played it right, we'd get the takings. And he pulled on an Indian rubber mask, because the manager knew him from drinking there, and this here Mr Castagne, a Frenchman would just hand everything over, and we'd split, off on our pilgrimage again. And I didn't know if I was too drunk or too sober to do it, so I went along, and Roman explains that with Castagne we can plead poverty, he'd throw the money at us, but if there was the English guy, though, that Mr Hardwick, we should talk tough and say we come from Montreal. As we walk back into town, he's fooling with the gun, and there must be something in there, and he blew out the rear window of a car, and I say, 'If we're sober, we're in trouble,' but he says it doesn't count, that here's a different time zone and among the rocks a brothel where the cops go, and sure enough we see a lot that's full of cruisers empty, just the radios clacking on like dead voices, and no one here is up to any good, just having fun.

And are we drunk or sober as we climb the stairs, and here's the manager's room, and Roman waves the gun about and says, 'We've made it – out in the open. The penalty for carrying a concealed weapon is extreme,' and he's got fixed on that word, extreme, and used it like a flag, and I think, 'He's proud! He's an idiot, but he's proud of what he's doing,' and I go along, to see what's happening, and if we get away, I have a chance of seeing Mad'len again, when her old man's off down the hole, and we are free and maybe rich. Besides, Roman's the only friend I have, and now I know him pretty well, though in his Indian mask he could be anyone.

And it is Mr Castagne, and he starts off, 'Yes, you boys, what can I do for you?' as if he's reading Mr Hardwick's lines, and he ignores the gun, or maybe doesn't want to see it, and he says to me, 'So, you an Indian, son? The hat, the hat, you know,' and I begin, 'No, no, an Indian gave—' but Roman waves the rifle, and Mr Castagne just sits, and I see he has a waitress or a secretary sitting there, and doesn't squawk or anything. And Mr Castagne has a hairpiece, slipping, slipping down in a decadent way, and it occurs to me, 'He's drunk,' and I want to laugh, because we are all three of us, all drunk, and maybe the secretary or waitress is even drunker, as she just says, 'Oh my', just once, 'Oh my.'

And Roman says, all thickly, 'Money, give the money. Give the money, and I'll tell you a secret. This here gun's not loaded.'

And I think, 'Here's something wrong, and after so many years of life, here's me and Roman giving a real poor, a stupid, show, just not to go down the mine, or watch the dust machine, or maybe brush up cinders with a burning brush.'

And Mr Castagne says, 'Well, now, you boys. You tell me your secret, and I'll tell you two. The first is – in this here drawer, I don't keep a gun, and so I can't blow your tails off. And the second,' and his hair slips off, so there is tension beneath what seems a humorous person, 'The cash is all downstairs. Those monkey waiters is still raking in and splitting all up between them. You should have waited round till later, maybe taken on another drink.'

And Roman says behind the mask, 'How could we wait, we're drunk already,' and I think we should give Mr Vapaus back his gun or there'll be trouble too, and Roman says to Mr Castagne that he is a real white man, though I think 'and a bald one too', and as we shuffle down the stairs I hear, 'Oh my' again.

The cops are out the front, and in the bar I see a black-blue thicket, cops all drinking. The place is full of guys going on the graveyard shift, or deciding they don't want to go, and so we find a table and sit there with a guy who says he was a mountie – married to an Indian woman somewhere in Manitoba, so he left the force. And he is our good conduct, so he says, and so we park the rifle by his chair, and he's too drunk to notice. And he's full of praise for Indians, saying they're the only people who don't want to take over the world, and that should make them like Canadians but it doesn't seem to, much, and perhaps the Indians own the world all along, though he finds the reservation uncomfortable, and his job got him laughed at, so we leave him, when Roman says he'll put me on the bus.

We make it to the bus station. It's full of Ukrainians. And I think that I shall never see Mad'len again, but at least another day and none of us has gone down the mine, and how labour made the country what it is, and that I should go North or South, but which? And Roman says the South, because there's more people, though it seems smaller.

He's talking away to the Ukrainians, and I say, 'I didn't know you were Ukrainian,' and he says, 'I'm all right, but what are you?' I lie and say, 'I'm a Polack', but I don't know what I am, and I don't care. He says, 'These old guys think they're going to be free one day,' and I say, 'Good for them.'

North? South? Better South.

He drops some acid. It was all a long time ago. He drops some acid, babbles of green fields, a world class of peaceful guys, leading us sheep somewhere, all weapons buried, and I remember Mr Vapaus's rifle – disappeared. Like the whole thing was a put up-job, for nothing. When the revolution comes, Mr Vapaus'll have to borrow a gun, just like we did.

I see the pools of green, black, brown water, a present immovable, savage. Value my lucidity, my reason, unemployment. Roman hallucinating – all that tequila.

The smelter peppers us with acid shot, like we are birds. I can get the bus at dawn, Mad'len doing her duty still, as she will come to wait in vain for me, her Northern knight. Heading South. And she was real honest, but a sad person. Wow, so sad.

A Ukrainian says, 'That hat there's Indian,' and I think, it kept me out the mine, and say, 'He gave me, you can take it, like I did. This Indian got it off an Indian too. A lucky hat,' and so, it goes. Rather, it stays, I go. And so that guy gets to be an Indian too. And maybe will find Mr Vapaus, in his roundabout way, saving him from death.

The hat, first having it, being recognised, then getting rid of it. When being recognised becomes a danger. Kept me from harm, saved from the dark mine, the fiery smelter. A damn shame, though, to lose a magic Indian hat.

Letting me slip, unruffled, as I step on to the bus, back into nature.

TRAVELS IN THE KIZZELKOOM

IT IS TIME for prayer. Some guy comes out on the balcony of the stubby minaret opposite our hotel window. He sounds off – not the usual tape, but a trumpet, cracking upwards at the last, three octaves of broken accidentals.

Sinclair is reading from his goddam guidebook again: 'Under the edges of the strata of ferruginous sandstone which cap the summit of Nogai-Kala are some caves frequented by owls of a very large size; and the unwary visitor is not unlikely to be upset and rolled down the steep slopes of the hill by the sudden flying out of the birds on his approach.' He rolls on his bed to face me with one dead-wolf yellow eye. 'Some times, those, Jay.'

He reminds me of a pustule, of Bolivar being carried through greater Colombia like a pustule, shedding his library, too goddam heavy, the library and the liberator both together.

'Tomorrow,' Sinclair says, scuffing at some insect bites and twisting in the styrofoam casing he uses in place of sheets, 'we go deeper. To what the Chinese called Zhou-Yen,' and he attempts a sing-song, 'and the Ayrabs Furruck-al-Ziy' – reading from the guidebook.

'What do we call it, Sinclair?' I ask. 'And no more mules.' Sinclair loping along in front, hanging over the mule's sides like a pair of saddlebags – a pair of saddlebags with thieves bundled in them.

He smiles horribly, and ladling Wisconsin on his Missouri says, 'Sure don't hear that mule complain.'

Companion, master, guide, and more than usual today – pustule. With his goddam guidebook, central Asia on fifty kopecks a day or suchlike goddam crap, and never knowing where we go, or where we want to go, or if we have arrived, what language or what country we are in – or even, maybe, are we looking for some other guys, or wanting to be friendly, how should I know, even sell them into slavery maybe, and Sinclair says, 'It's all come down, you see. It's all gone back to how it was, and we're two flies, or spiders maybe, sidling along the crack where China and the Ayrabs meet the Turks, and then you see, the Mongols,' and at that word he pauses, like he's crossing himself, or maybe making an evil-eye sign, or thinking of piles of skulls a hundred metres high, higher than the Golden Gate, a sliding zone that never stops, and I'm quite desperate now, I ask, 'What we goddam looking for, man?' – and see his face go bronzy and I soften it all up and add, 'Sinclair, old man, old friend.'

He sweeps along, as if he's ordering foreign troops about – 'And then, young Jay, I have my little theory that when the Greeks got to the river, well – what Greek would ever stop and draw a line, and say – "thus far"? Arriving at the Oxus,' he rears up and starts poking in his Samsonite, 'Wherever at that time it may have been, where would they have gone but down it? Meeting, you know, the Scythians, and later on, Chinese. And then voyaging for years, decades, for generations, through Chinese villages. And towns. And provinces. Where the river goes, young Jay.'

'It goes nowhere, Sinclair.'

He says, impatiently, 'Other rivers, there's always other rivers. That goddam river don't go anywhere, young Jay, because you're going round the handling of it wrong. It's already finished. In the West, it flows into the sea. Or out of it. But always going east, you see, they find more rivers. So, one generation, they will reach another sea.'

'But Sinclair, they don't want to find another one. They want home.'

'Home is relative, Jay.' He turns his samoyed eye on me, he laughs, 'Jay, home is *relatives*.'

'Sinclair, it's where I want to go. Not my home, necessarily, just someone's home.'

He dismisses it with a flap of his hand. 'And truth, Jay? Values? All that Berkeley crap?'

'Outmoded, Sinclair, and I never graduated.'

'Graduated? Sure as fuck you didn't graduate. How could a guy like you graduate when you got your crummy job in the parking lot stacking the young scholars' automobiles?'

He makes an attitude with a towel, as if it's a toga. 'The Romans, now, young Jay, you'll find them along behind, wherever two Greeks have gone a thousand of your Romans follow – down the road to China too. Or maybe India. Or just stay here, fight in the desert, go to the Urals, what the fuck should I care,' he finishes irritably. It is very hot. We are covered with blotchy bites, we look fat and white and grey like two flatfish.

Sinclair asks, quite kindly, 'How's the shamanism going?'

'I can't ease out my long-bones the way they should. The rest is all quite simple.'

'Visiting the dead? And dying?'

'A cinch.'

He says, 'Well, keep on taking lessons. There is a knack to everything – and since we're here, you should try the "speshaltay of the may-zon".' He laughs, and I think, 'He's a great man, yes, a pustule, but a great, a very great man indeed,' and he brings out the stuff he's hunted for: 'You see this, Jay? You see it, can you name it? Can you sell it?'

'It's a gunsight, Sinclair.'

'It's a gunsight, it's a gunsight,' he scoffs, and capers round the room. 'What these guys here would want with gunsights, poor buggers shooting at poor buggers, don't need a gunsight to sight yourself, you fool.' He is excited, and he screeches, 'History, you fool! It's all come down, you fool. The world is on the move, the movement of the peoples starts again.' He breathes into my face, 'Islam is the last. Last night' – he grips me – 'Last night I met someone, eyes like walled gardens. They were ready. They inclined their ear. And I put' – he is delighted, high – 'and I put my tongue deep, deep into Islam.'

He stands back. 'You want my reaction, Sinclair?' I ask.

'Sure, why not. To you, I'm just a pustule. But you know, I am your teacher. I am a great man, a very great pustule, Jay. And though it hurt to do it, I can lead men, have led men. Outmoded, maybe. But up the hill, not fearing owls.'

I say primly, 'Islam is obedience to the truth, Sinclair,' and quietly he says, 'The truth, Jay, is outmoded. And history is the thing.'

He presses the gunsight against my eye. I can see eyelid. Then blood and tears.

I say, 'Jesus, Sinclair, what's in this thing?'

'The future and the past, dear boy. My history scope.'

'The present?'

'I'm having difficulty calibrating that, dear boy.'

I ask, 'You plan to sell this stuff, then, Sinclair?'

He says haughtily, 'Not sell the merchandise, young Jay. I sell a look, a peep. Forward or back. The present, Jay,' he whispers in my face again, his breath smells of walled gardens, 'The present, Jay, has fallen down into itself. It really doesn't count.'

'Sinclair, you don't need insist with me. It's the American way, I guess, the present and all that, but if your gadget doesn't pick it up, it's all the same to me.'

He looks at me suspiciously. 'Well, I hope you're right. The guys round here are funny. On the move. The big religions, all that stuff, come in like earthquakes, like gods with nuclear mowers,' and he reads from the guide, '"when night closed in, this sea without ships and these shores without ports assumed a sadness which was all their own, as a nebulous mist veiled the starlight and spread like a pall over waters whose ripples gave out no gleam of phosphorescence". Wow, Jay, some writing. Some place.'

'But Sinclair, everything is coming down. Those communist guys, that fucking trumpeter on the minaret, and countries that aren't countries, and just go on, we don't know what the goddam place is called because the guide's a century old …' and Sinclair is furious, he shouts, 'More than a century, you fool. You whine, you whine. Did the Greeks whine, when they were led on and on, deep into …' he searches for words like where we are now at: 'People. Things. Villages. Shamans. Where you go down, and there's an unstoppered jar, and thousands more jars stoppered that you mustn't touch', and I'm surprised – 'Sinclair, only shamans can go down there and back', and he is silent.

*

It is hot. It is cold. We travel through villages, towns once full of walled gardens, grey dust plains, grey mud plains. Sometimes we fly in planes over this landscape of old scarred skin, sitting side by side like two magicians on the same carpet. Sometimes I run along behind Sinclair on his mule, shouting 'Teach me everything I know, then,' but the wind blows away the irony, and we are closed in by four winds, one of sand and one of dust, one of mica, one of bronze, and everything the guidebook says falls far below the truth.

I ask Sinclair, 'You think we'll sell the gunsight?' and he replies, all haughty now – 'Well, you see, my dear young friend, as a gunsight it may not be so hot, but as history – what a portent,' and I gather that he dropped the fucking thing, or trod on it somehow, and all I ask myself is what the fuck I'm doing here, and knowing truth only so as to submit to it is a poor reward for being dead and going down there, and seeing all the goddam dead and stuff like that, and maybe legions Sinclair has abandoned here among the dunes during his passages, and on the goddam fat bastard goes, and he's ranting all the time about the commissars we meet, about the guy who played great trumpet on the minaret, about whoever's ear he got his tongue in, or time as the skin that holds the cosmic organs in, and all that crap I got at Berkeley, and I ask: 'Sinclair, when you going to let me go?' and he rages at me, 'What it is, you got nowhere to go, so I get to take you. A man should travel free, not with some goddam hippy on a string,' and maybe he is right, for sure as hell I don't know where we're going, the places being changed each day, and sometimes Sinclair asking for the ticket in Chinese, and sometimes Arabic and sometimes pure Manhattan, and he's asking to see imams and gunrunners all the time, but specially if they've been what he calls 'those old commie guys', and we get ourselves some nasty corners, and one time I have to do a footrace in the desert – the prize is if I lose, castration, and if I win – then nothing, and off you go rejoicing.

And yet, what these guys all see is what I know: that Sinclair is a great man. A very great, a very lasting man. Beside Sinclair, just being dead or living is a pretty trivial thing, and Sinclair says, 'I am the glue. I am the everlasting gum that puts these broken bits together,' and one day we find a bar and in the back are all the broken pool cues in the world, and I say to Sinclair, 'Why don't you try to mend this fucking lot,' and he says wisely, that they must go somewhere and then wait their turn.

'Let me go,' I say. 'Let's go,' and he says quite gently, 'I'm not a humanist, you know, young Jay.' But to show his trust in me, I get to carry the Samsonite with all the money in, that it comes from somewhere I don't want to ask, and he takes on the suitcase with his dirty socks in, and I think maybe I've made a step towards obedience, or it may be truth, and I even think one of those goddam winds that look like walls is maybe a bit opaque, and then they overbook us on some flight, and it's Sinclair on the mule again, and more melons, tea and these goddam castles built of mud, and piles of skulls a hundred metres high that turn out as pylons or maybe radio-towers as you come up to them.

And Sinclair is busy squinting at his gunsight, and he shows it to all kinds of guys, some are in suits and some in frocks, and some I'll swear are Chinese, and some piss down straws, and Sinclair whispers to me that that is real old time, and even in Missouri, in his youth ...

And Sinclair tells them all he's not a humanist, and sometimes asks them where the sea is, sometimes which way the rivers flow, and sometimes lets them use the history scope, and sits there like a happy seal and watches as they click it to and fro.

And there are cops and frontiers, and some days we change our money and get copper slugs or little rolls of mud, or perfume on our wrists, and Sinclair coins a slogan,

'You don't smell, so we won't sell' and for a while it seems he'll start an advertising scam in Kungrad; on this occasion he is much impressed with all the lovely women, but who knows what the place is called today and besides, as Sinclair says, sensations pall, that's what they're meant to do. Kindly he asks me how the shamanism is going, and if I want to start a parlour or a circle when I get back home, and so I tell him how you really need for roasting off your flesh and binding up the bones with copper wire – is lots of coke, but nothing like that here, they sell you nutmeg, and he laughs and says how I'm a ragamuffin, how I live 'without even ideal wealth, and therefore living on the interest from the capital of your opinion', and I say that's very well, but if I've nothing much to offer, at least I've got something big to hunt. And then he smiles and looks away, and taps the Samsonite with all the bucks.

*

And so we travel on, this must be China, even though the guys here do Turkish wrestling, and I see Sinclair ogling them as they oil up with cornseed oil from old UNRA cans. A sadness is heavy here, they do not seem to seek the truth, like me, nor do they have a Sinclair to obey, and even Sinclair seems disturbed, though not downhearted, which he cannot be, so long as I am here. And he sing-songs:

'These cities were once set out here like jewels along a river. Now, it's dust. But I shall make these buggers rise again. I'll make them great.'

'They'll get stomped, Sinclair,' I tell him, but he won't be stopped.

'No, Jay, I'll make them more than great, I'll make them frightening.'

'It's all been tried, Sinclair, and our guys just laughed.'

He's really angry now, he bangs the history scope down on the floor, and screams, 'Our side? Our guys? You foolish guy, you foolish friend, it's all gone down again, it's dancing off, it's twirling into dust. Nobody's got *our* guys, *our* good old guys, *our* side—' and I must interrupt and say, 'Sure they have, Sinclair,' but he rushes on, and says, 'What you call our side, young Jay, what they most afraid of, real afraid, and not the blacks and not the poor, and not the reds which now there isn't any, and not the judgement which there may be but who gives a fuck? Eh? I want your answer, seeker after truth.' His breath is close to mine: it smells of nutmeg.

I've no clue, I've no idea. It could be anything: the mafia, maybe, or jiggers, a blowout on the freeway, how should I know?

'The Mongols,' Sinclair says, and stands back, pleased. 'I'll mobilise the Mongols.' So that is why we came. I'm really moved.

'The Europeans will just blast them, Sinclair,' I say. 'With nuclear cannons.'

He muses. 'With nuclear cannons, eh?' And then he brightens, 'Then we'll find them something more, maybe,' but he's thoughtful. 'I never thought. So that's why every general needs a shaman. Thank you, Jay, you done a real good turn.' He's really impressed with me, my faith in him is rocked. Over and over he repeats, 'The Mongols. Blasted with nuclear cannons. Invasion over. The Mongols ... '

I sidle out the room. I nearly take the Samsonite with all the bucks, but in the end, take nothing. Go out on the street.

Nothing on the street. Just lots of guys waiting. A bookstore selling one familiar book, there must be thousands of them, *Central Asia* ... I hide from Sinclair. 'The gloom of the West Turkestan steppes, which first impresses one so forcibly in the Karakoom deserts North of Aral, seems surpassed by the sadness of the Kizzelkoom ... As the vision passes from ghastly-looking ridges of sand that are sprinkled with funereal-looking bushes, over immense stretches of lifeless-looking, bare, clay plains which are lost in a low continuous line of elevations on the horizon, the feeling of novelty aroused by such surroundings is almost overcome by a sense of mysterious awe ...'

I go out on the street, and there's a group of ragged commissars, they greet me, they are pleased to see a friend of Sinclair's, they're delighted – and I break away, I run. I run and as I pass the inn where we were staying, I see Sinclair in a sharkskin suit, he hasn't seen me but he's on a high again, he's gathering his legions. Oh and now he's seen me and he opens wide his arms, he pops his tongue out and I'm at the door, I run up to him.

And I pass him, and I keep on running.

BLACK MASKS

Même à Minas Velhas, la vie nouvelle
a ses attraits: un jour, elle
bousculera tout cet ordre ancien,
fragile, qui s'y maintient par miracle.

F. Braudel, Dans le Brésil bahianais

1   *Black Masks*

I AM SITTING in a bar in New York. Outside it is raining. It is suddenly dark: then day again. They are singing Brazilian songs – one Brazilian song. They have brought with them some of their blue insects – eyes garnet, or jade, pale jade, green flesh of fruit. The song is about the 'Trumpet Wheel'. It is light, then dark again. Voices probing and rude, probing secret parts. A set-up. Something not quite right, like lanes of traffic just off colour – orange, indigo, food in fashion colours moving on the plate: kedgeree and apricots, swarmed with crickets, copper and billon: eyes on stalks, flakes of silver or tinfoil. Windows all smoked up – yellow outside too bright for forsythia, must be plastic. All-American loot. Definitely a set-up, waiting to be skinned. Hear a Venetian 'x', sounds like something coming from long black noses under long black masks.

Hear them saying '*sim, sim*', always two jumps, two yesses, ahead. We know, have already thought that, destroyed all prevision. Cleverness of people very rich and very poor, room only for every extreme.

I am obsessed by carnival. A universe, a history, a continent with no structure, no end, save carnival. No god, state, class, just a thousand processions, seven days of wrap-around cinema. No family, no Oedipus. When I first landed in Rio, I was instantly robbed, all my papers, my shoes. I had to invent a plausible past, a new, paper-thin identity. But it was not Rio that obsessed me, it was Bahia.

You can't sell carnival, as they did in Venice. But we outsiders look for many disparate things in carnival – certainly not display or conformity, but many small things, not the thing itself. My obsession does not begin with the people, the people of Bahia. It comes from the struggle to be free of jungles, jungles that mean very little because they are less penetrable, more contorted, than any human soul or situation. At the rim of every jungle there is a carnival, the authentic face, the living mask, the life beyond the jungle. And then, certainly, the people, the estuary, freeing from river, dissolving into sea – a dangerous condition.

Travelling often, I am an easy target for witchcraft; can't find my own antidotes, my own witches. It all depends on yourself, your own signs, formulas, twists of paper. The people you bring with you are changed – become sleepy, stupid, aggressive. Where I usually live, we have a balance, a field of force, a truce: men and women, people and animals, circumstance and happenstance. Precarious and vulnerable from the outside – forces taking people away, destroying the usefulness of the horse and donkey – selling carnival. Forces you must respect. But they disrupt the magic of the everyday – not looking at the mountains in May, not facing East when talking to people. Not magic, just ease; comfort, even.

In New York, here on neutral, indifferent ground, I muster round my magic. Two Brazilians watch me. '*Sim, sim,*' they say.

They said New York was a good place; you lied to come in, not to go out. Usually it was the reverse. They had a friend, a lover, in Rome. They wanted me to greet her for them. 'What should I say?' 'Naturally, whatever you wish.'

Yes, yes, they were from Bahia. Of course I lived near Rome. Of course their friend was easy to find, Rome was an orderly, a civil city; yes, yes, very *religious*, very lawful.

For Brazilians they were old; thirty-five. Carnival days nearly done. I liked them immensely. We drank together. The light changed. I returned to Rome, without telling more lies.

In my village, carnival time returned, and memories of my marginal commitment came back too – the lover from Bahia. The corners of her piazza were *trompe l'oeuil*. No church, just an eternal flame to Stendhal – one of his three-week Roman lodgings. Buildings were ochre, cocoa, Amazon mud, façades alien to the apartments, in style and by decades. Buildings stronger than the Romans; built by those the Romans had inveigled in. Romans too had paid others to put on a bloody carnival. Problem of rubbish disposal: 'His excellency, president of the street, promises a black eye and a whipping to anyone depositing dead or partial animals, unredeemed gaming tokens, false saints, bad jokes, on or near the public way.' A long corridor, a kitchen of the 1930s, many rooms where people of the '60s might be sleeping, or simply have moved on. I ask:

'You are from Bahia?'

'Recife.'

'Your friends?'

'I think from Recife.'

I felt entirely at my ease.

'I've brought some of our wine. It's strong. We put a snake in it to make it strong.'

'Yes, yes.'

In fact we put copper in – but sometimes snakes; one year a neighbour went to put gunpowder in his vinegar, and found it a mass of worms.

I say, 'Italy has never had really indigenous inhabitants. So we are always comparing customs. In the next village they go round every morning collecting urine – for the washing.'

'Yes, yes. But it is a hard place to make money.'

'Are people here interested in Brazil?'

'Yes, yes. But they muddle up the countries. Then, what does it matter?' Yes, yes, I thought, and you have carnival.

In the Americas, closest point to Rome is Brazil. There, they have carnival to keep them together. Up North here, only the philosophy of the corner store. A marginal observation that, I'd have said in more political days. But now, the idea of carnival was enough to make erotic resonances: point to larger, even menacing, relations and responsibilities. Even the free can't resist a call to freedom. And here, in this narrow, clerical Rome – a city like a rich, ravaged, senile aunt, miserly with cash and touched about religion – no, certainly, one never felt free.

'Yes, yes. But *village* carnival?'

I told her about the original peoples, living – at least in my imagination and theirs – outside the city. 'In Rome there's just barbarians. They made the ruins and boast about how beautiful it is to live in them. The indigenous people live all around.'

'Yes. This is very conservative.'

She handled the coffee cups like finger-cymbals. Much later she said, 'You understand yourself quite well.' The only direct observation she ever made about me. We talked about the hinterland of Recife.

'Jaguars, yes. A musty smell. But not in the cities. And here?'

'Occasionally a small wild beast – escaping. My friends – some from the Austrian embassy, sailors with Nansen passports, bodyguards, organists, good gipsies. Trustworthy people, tough.'

'Not just exotics, then?' The coffee was muddy.

'Yes. That is musty too – perhaps the water?'

I felt solid and well-protected. She asked: 'Why did you like my friends?'

'Because I thought they were from Bahia. And yet there was something wrong. But in New York—'

'You expected a mystery. And yet, like many, they are probably just desperate.'

We spoke about my city friends. 'Together,' I said, 'they don't make up, let's say, a renaissance: rather, continuous creation. You know that Bruno was burnt for that? His most disturbing idea.'

The point seemed academic.

'Yes, yes. And are you subversive as well?'

'We live the best way, by expedients. Not being subordinate, that's the trick: nothing fixed.'

'Yes. But my expedients don't work so well. That's their snag.'

'You need friends – what the Romans called a cult.'

'Yes, of course. But cults devoted to expediency? The modern thing, for sure?'

'Single women have an awkward role. And then, too many think they're witches, and that breaks up our circle.'

'Yes, it would. But – "single women" – are there other kinds?'

'A manner of speaking. Or describing.'

She decided to come with me to the village carnival, though what her friends had wanted of me, what she wished, was indefinite. We left the gates of Rome to the South and passed into the harder-edged air of Etruria.

We stopped at a necropolis. Pig country; now the hunters would massacre them. Streets of the dead; trees temporarily retreated. Tufa colour of grain; unstoppered tombs, and even bones. Familiar broad-seriffed porticoes. The family tombs with dining areas for the survivors to visit. Or maybe for the dead to take the summer air. Steps cut for the damp ghosts, drying off, raising black beakers, picking figs, a rose. Faint oakwood smoke, dogs chiming together like church towers; hunters' guns. A russet donkey, absent-minded but insistent; shepherds running like goats. She said:

'Many dead.'

'They felt death involved more permanency than life, could take stronger constructions.'

'They were right.'

Here, any mystery had been expended, all relations drained. All tension worked out, place given over to nothing.

'What do we do at the carnival? Watch, like a procession?'

'It's not Recife. And there's no music.' Something not right here. A mistake, perhaps; details blurred. Carnival become a high frieze, dead flicker of New York, electric particles trapped in tubes.

Village with ramparts of gingerbread tufa, streets palmed away and ridged for transport of grapes. Horses with cowboy saddles outside the bar. Cowboys. Cowboys and cowboys' uncles in Fiats. 'Yes, yes.'

Lost bandsmen. Tall back-legs of horses, corseted, all taken up a notch. 'You know all these people?' she asks.

'Yes, of course.'

'A real Etruscan.' She's serious.

With us, carnival is an archaeology of fears and fantasies – horsemen dressed as Turks, riderless horses racing down the main street, and here, in the home of the anti-Jove, the god of disfavours, we have a procession 'in reverse'. A travesty of everyday, an inversion of the normal hierarchy.

'Yes, yes. Usually you have poor lawyers and rich peasants, today the rich peasants play the lawyers and so on?'

'In a way. People trust themselves to a disguise. They wear it for a time while their normal powers are suspended. Women dress as men, townsmen as, peasants, riders walk. You tempt your fates, but take care to be well disguised.'

'And is this funny or terrible?'

'It recognises precariousness.'

'Yes, but it seems there must be something more.'

One year a horse broke its leg as it raced, when the entrance to a tomb subsided. Behind us, they were discussing whether it was bones or muscles that were full of blood.

'Really, I hate carnival,' she said. 'With us, it's not clear, not open. It covers *nothing*, conceals nothing – nothingness. And it's violent. In a way, it's hell, even though it's "in my blood". Too much reality. But this, in your village – this is a trick. No one really goes down to hell, the gods aren't fooled. And I think by now the Etruscans know their destiny.'

We – Etruscans – had revived carnival when other paths, other futures, seemed blocked. Young people stay away. They're a different tribe. Less intense, less tortuous. And with our charade, we've closed ourselves to them.

Luisa and I watched more races, bands, travesties. A week later, the village had resumed its usual forms, planting its feet in different millennia, saving face with unreasonable confidence.

That spring, the political economy of magic fitted quite well with that of expedients. Luisa, my 'lover from Bahia', and I were often together. The things unexplained were outweighed, mostly, by explanation of the contingent. The 1930s kitchen became dingier as the sun became more intense; the coffee tasted of copper and cat fur, but thus became a joke. I felt our carnival had troubled her – it seemed for her a carnival of Northern peasants, almost Bavarian, miners and woodsmen, goldsmiths and forest clearings. But she never admitted to disappointment – just occasional preoccupations, irritations. Her 'expedients' were not permitted to threaten her autonomy. Friends – now our friends – went North or abroad to work, to bring back money, sometimes to avoid short prison terms. Defence of shared traditions did not seem, as she had said, 'very conservative', nor yet demanding.

Magic had, in fact, replaced larger projects and perspectives. Rome became neither a Soviet republic, nor did it seem to nurture new Rienzis, nor anti-Rienzis, in the crowds that passed from shoe-shop to shoe-shop on weekend afternoons, youths and their pretty, aimlessly free girlfriends from the periphery. Too much traffic for riderless horse races, though it was again legal to wear masks, during carnival. Luisa made few comments: 'We have carnival because we're desperate.'

There is something not quite right. Everyone is leaving the city, which is filling with non-people, tourists. The cause is the summer; but there must be another reason for abandoning one's home, one's terrain. Even the village emptied; the season – if it was that – took Luisa. She stayed away. The fields turned to ochre, to dust, lifted off as clouds.

*

I am sitting in a bar in New York. It is bitterly cold for a place this far uptown. Outside there is a jungle heat. My Brazilians come in. They are evidently discussing a deal. They have struggled, perhaps for days, to get this far uptown. Other Brazilians are singing – 'Poor Cow': now, I understand the words and music better, differently. It was on one of Luisa's records. 'Always punctual', the Brazilians say. I tell them, 'I was punctual yesterday too – that was the day we were to meet.'

We talk about Luisa: 'Yes, yes, she makes an impression.'

I tell them she and I are for different reasons not in Rome: 'yes, yes.' They sound impatient: they manage to be impatient for days. The light begins to come and go, perhaps days pass as it changes. They have aged considerably in this year: at thirty-six, they have the poise of ancients. Juliao explains that he and Luisa were lovers years ago: and Nicolao – 'him too, but at different times. Perhaps we shall be again.' Someone has brought a jaguar. There is a musty smell – or it may be camphor. The jaguar, too, maybe a dog with an expensive collar. Juliao's crucifix has a Christ with red, garnet eyes.

I do not feel solid, at ease. Nicolao is talking about systems: at first I think it is a numbers game. 'Yes, yes. New systems.'

I say: 'The symbols the numbers represent change from place to place.'

'No, I mean something different.'

The cat on the bar is fishing with its paw in a jug of dusty water. Nicolao says, 'We have met again. We make up a system which as yet has no purposes, no finalities. But it's solid, it spreads. It stands up to passion, interests I wouldn't tell to everyone, things not quite respectable. Yet this isn't a simple system, like in the past, when I build an automobile, become an auto-worker, struggle alongside my comrades. Am a slave, am beaten. Live in Rome, am a Roman. Read Marx, look on the world with revolutionary eyes. No, the old systems are still there, but you see that we are part of new ones. We don't believe we can free ourselves of the old, just to end up remaking them under different names: slaves becoming slavemasters, with all the power of the old – only without slaves. We don't believe that any more.'

Our drinks are bitterly cold. Air-conditioning roars.

I remember Luisa saying 'they are desperate', or was it 'we are desperate'? Systems sound like business, expedients. What makes up Luisa's system?

Juliao is saying, 'You can accept these new systems passively – they are walls that move aside. You have mobility, even in your mind. If you can read, you read a book, or a scrap of paper and you are a citizen of the world. If you can't read, the radio tells you a hundred ways to be freer, more responsible. And nothing really changes: you leave your kids, they're still hungry. You leave Brazil and in New York they call you honky or nigger. Or you can use these systems pos-it-ively.'

I ask, 'Like a chain letter?'

Juliao turned the glowing Christ eyes against his skin. 'Everything sounds like a scam. Carnival's the biggest scam there is – all year and every year. I'm telling you – the old rules don't apply: they can't apply. Or, they apply quite arbitrarily. People in New York get eaten by jaguars and alligators, kids from the jungle play pro hockey in Copenhagen.'

'So?'

'Yes. So, you want poor kids to get ahead; and one of them makes a million bucks with "Poor cow", or whatever. Can you wait for that to happen, to get the credit, the satisfaction? May as well play the lottery: all these things are organised like the lottery now. What you need is a little system, part of a big system outside the rules, where you have a good time losing – even winning.'

Desperate.

Juliao has given up explaining. He is older, richer, darker than Nicolao. 'Nicolao, yes. Nicolao can always get you drinks. He can charm snakes. Only snakes. Useful in New York.' Nicolao looks furtive, the clever boy overly devious. He wants to be more convincing. He wears no gold. Place him: prison and horses. I too don't wear gold; making money out of horses bores me: I tell him, 'Horses is a dangerous business: too many two-legged runners,' he agrees and gets more icy drinks.

Nicolao ponderously outlines schemes: horses, films, a band of dancers, Brazilian culture, tourism.

'Small profits, big losses,' I say, and Juliao seems more cheerful. He talks of his family, left behind in Gary.

'Gary, Indiana?'

'A very catholic city. The best place to leave a family.'

It seems we are to be part of Luisa's system, whatever she makes it. I like Juliao and Nicolao immensely, but the figures, and the symbols they represent – a black ballet, structuralists from Rio, Indian medicines – are overpowering. We must have sat here for a week: the other Brazilians are singing 'Trumpet Wheel'. What is it here that is not right – aside from the times, the temperatures? Remember the drinking games – games no longer played in the village, because they lead to deaths. The 'prince' decides who shall drink, who shall be excluded, and the 'courtiers' group in factions, excluding, enforcing sobriety or drunkenness. We are certainly not playing for money. Is this the system? Seeking the secret friend, presupposing the secret enemy; being part of someone else's game, but capable of winning it – that is, of in turn becoming prince, master of the mystery, of the game's power, but not its hierarchy, its ordering?

Juliao and Nicolao, then, are enemies, and Luisa is part of the game only incidentally – not being bound by the rules, and free to leave, and not to play. I share the passion for the game, but each must have another passion; mine is carnival, and that they know – but carnival not as scam, and now they know that too. They hate each other enough to make Luisa part of the game, expanding the system. This gives them reason to hate me; or to need me; or to love me. I'm in the same condition, so I must untangle the real hatred from the game, and its rules. But the game itself is not a pretext: it is a reason, an occasion, for hatreds, for alliances. Too much, or too little: drinking or thirst. Juliao prince over Nicolao, or the reverse. The pretext, once, perhaps Luisa, or horses. More likely another game, another spectacle – horses. If it were only Luisa, would I have entered? Bringing me in raised the stakes, extended the game, resolved nothing. The game produces its own pretexts. The final demolishing drink, the pistol slipped to you, the loan pressed on you – as destructive as their strategic withholding. And after all, they were Brazilians.

Perhaps, indeed, with my own carnival, I had become the prince – prince ignorant of his courtiers. I had arrived first: I – perhaps – held the cards, the luck, the magic, the order, the power. Now, we are playing, and we know we're in the game.

Digging into Juliao was digging mud, into Nicolao, sand. In Juliao there was an archaeology of wood, monsters still fleshed, a dragging stickiness of memory. Nicolao was bones and shards, glass becoming mica, mica once more sand. Juliao forgot no slight, but he was sluggish with rancours. Nicolao treasured petty kindnesses, but he had the mind and memory of a provincial lawyer. They had nothing left but the game, no loyalties save to the fall of the invisible cards.

They were like tramps or millionaires – fallen down or wafted up to the same condition, knowing rather than liking the other. Mature men, they call us; heavy with our maturity, evening-drinking lions. Capable of any past, but not now, in ourselves, interesting. It's carnival, the game; game and reality can't be separated, why should they be?

They're desperate. Always gaming, like the poor become rich.

'Yes, yes. Politics. Very dangerous for us. The territory is too large, the spaces in it too narrow.' They laugh at the idea of being boss, or dogsbody; who laughs louder?

'What space is left for us?'

We drink more frozen drinks.

Juliao becomes heavier, darker. Nicolao complains of the cold and says, 'Too damn low-key in here.' Stalking, hunting, calling to the musicians. He has reversed the air-conditioning. 'Bring a bit of the outside inside.' The manager protests, tries to throw him out. It is becoming torrid inside. Probably the outside is unaffected.

Juliao says: 'He was in the jungle, you know. When they built Brasilia. A real *worker*, with a hardhat.' Perhaps he is joking. 'He loved that place. Built the most luxurious slum in the world. Built it on the backs of alligators. Scared of them, is Nicolao. Sees them in his sleep. A real fighter, but he's afraid to use his gun now.' He is trying to fight the manager. Juliao uses the increase in tension to confide: 'Luisa has been his woman. But she doesn't care any more, now he's been in the jungle. Just another roughneck.' I wonder – in the jungle, or in jail? Jail in Brazil spoils you for many things. Juliao pushes me down on the table in his effort to make me hear: 'She doesn't exist. Not there.'

Nicolao is shouting to the manager about the jungle: the musicians are inspired by the near-fighting. Everyone is much happier. Nicolao skimming ashtrays off tables to break against the walls; like skipping stones off alligators on mudflats or shallows. There is feeble talk of the police.

Nicolao says: 'I bought the police when I bought your ice-balls' – and the trumpet player laughs. Nicolao laughs too. He pulls out a patrimony of bills. Juliao says, 'They won't give him a credit card.' He pays for more days and nights of song; the band is delighted, people come in and try to dance, but it's too hot. We feel sober but malarial.

Juliao winks at me: 'No more drinks for *him*.'

*

I am sitting in a bar, in New York, with Luisa. I do not expect to see Juliao and Nicolao, and cannot imagine seeing either separately from the other. The last time, we left the bar in a taxi that had been waiting for us. Nicolao said, 'Juliao always has a friend with a taxi wait outside. He feels more secure.' Juliao said no, he was just lazy; drivers didn't come that far uptown. The driver, his friend, had been reading – for how many days? – a child's book about insects. Some had been roughed-in with blue ballpoint.

Luisa said, 'So, I'll be coming back to Rome. We shall be together there.'

'I'm glad.'

A very white girl was dancing: the tune was 'Blue Butterfly'. 'Very white people seem anomalous in the world now.' Luisa changed a hundred and compared the identical fifties for a long time. 'I like to think the Etruscans weren't as white as Romans always are in school books.'

I say: 'Her body is bluer than the butterfly's.' The light changed, or seemed to change, to gold, to day. She spoke of Juliao: 'He's always slowly moving. Like mud, you know.'

'I know.'

She went on: 'Nicolao, though, is spent, he'll never manage anything more.'

'He never spoke about you. Juliao did.'

She laughed. 'They want to keep tabs on me.' I asked if she minded that.

'It irritates me, but if they don't care, one could be dead. And they are desperate, you know.'

'Juliao has his family in Gary – does that make him desperate too?'

'He has no family that I know of. He can't go back anywhere. He and Nicolao don't even use their Brazilian names here. For Juliao, when he talks of going back, he means staying here, in New York. He hates to leave. He always makes a bad relationship.'

I said I didn't know, didn't suspect that.

'How would you?' she said.

She talked of carnival. 'Carnival is as you imagine it, exactly. Everything else is different from how you see it. Richer, but mostly poorer. And more desperate. And even when you lift a black mask, you may find nothing underneath. Or a country face, like yours. I dread carnival, it's like an open wound.'

'Because it's startling and disgusting? Is that why you dislike it? Or because it's a game without winners?'

'There sure as hell are winners. Don't believe otherwise. But winning brings responsibilities, other people depend on you, on your power. With village magic, you all stay private and alone as you were before. Carnival magic lasts all year: it gives power which makes you sore; or gives you dependency which you resent.'

'Shan't we be seeing Nicolao or Juliao?'

'Yes, yes. They're not here. But I've plans for you.' Not everyone can be planned for: it requires an availability which pleases me when I consider my prospects.

They are playing 'King Congo'; flattering, the words, or vainglorious. Arrogance of the freed slave. Carnival takes time to sediment. 'My own ancestors were hit-and-run pirates,' and she answers, 'History is sad, everywhere sad. It teaches us only – that history is sad.'

'We can say "a sad song", but not "a sad crowd". Perhaps that's why I crave carnival.'

'Yes, yes. But forget about carnival, and think about what people want you to do. Cut cane, for example.'

'We must hate the past. And all its networks.'

'Yes, yes.'

'And the present, which pretends this hatred can't exist.'

'Yes, yes. But hatred is out of fashion. Too bad for me.'

And yet, for Juliao, swallowing everything, this hatred means she doesn't exist. Or else it is a trick.

I am bored with the drinking, bored with the music which is made of coloured glass, stale patchouli, trombone studies for the conservatoire. Bored with an Africa that exists only in music.

'Not only in music. And what else do they have? What else do we have.'

She buys a drink I don't want. 'Where were you when you left Rome?' I ask.

'I saw Nicolao and Juliao.' I had not thought of that. It was a shock. It did not answer the question.

Rome has moved quite far from Africa: smug with owning no more slaves, gone out of fashion. Luisa leans forward to catch what she may suspect to be an important statement. I buy another drink: 'Too damn low-key.' At least she and I are comrades, as the game puts it. We both expect Nicolao and Juliao to come in. We have been waiting for them for three days, or it may be more. But then, I was a day late. Who knew when Luisa had arrived. New York seemed the intersection of two great circles, floating round each other like lily pads on a lake: circles centred on places – Italy, Brazil. We four like bright insects taken for a ride. I buy another drink. I am feeling very solid. 'Where did you see our friends this summer?'

'We were in Bahia.'

2   *The Bahians*

HE TOOK his field-report from the big map case, whose spiked foot he set in a patch of wild radishes. 'Yes, this says pretty much where I'm at.' We went back into the darkness to measure the dimensions of the warrior and his wife. To me, the alcoves further in held little messes of goat bones, burnt, or they might be dog. But he said firmly, 'Servants. Pelvises all broken up.'

The police helicopters above searched for authentic tomb robbers. We unfurled our sun umbrellas, pink and white, and printed with our scholars' numbers. Big ants made tracks. 'I always hope to find a spaceship, some galactic cowboys with the gift of resurrection, rattling the old bones back into some orgy.'

He looked at me as though he were trying to tune a faded radio with his eyes: 'What you call orgies were really communions, but with the sexual part left in.'

'Exactly.'

He loped ahead. Brazilians know what they're looking for: at archaeology, we're just Martians, distinguishing rocks and measuring. Carlos said again, as often, 'Knew how to live in many modes at once. Not just importing things from other places, but brought their gods, their drugs, civilisation – all that. Doesn't mean they travelled authentically, or lasted better. Rather, they saw time like an artichoke, themselves as a leaf – specific only as part of a whole growing ever denser round them. Dominant imagery and science – the passage of water through rocks: decanting sacrificial blood down basalt runnels. Science all dried out by Romans. Christians caught some of it, perhaps, in catacombs – but only a waft, tame stuff. Airless, soundproof, sterile.'

Most summers, many Bahians came to Rome. Hardly had the TV finished its tripping at carnival – this year three thousand facsimiles of Jeanette MacDonald clones from Drumnadrochit to Rio – than the first of them arrived. So far this year, only Carlos had come, seeking like the others his 'expedients', hinting at affairs gone suddenly desperate, social fabrics holed and gaping, illusions once more boringly sundered.

Spell I couldn't break – Bahians telling me with assurance things not new, not unknown: 'That's your problem, spells you can't break', said Luisa, my lover from Bahia who had begun it all, succession of vivid braggarts, desperate, despairing, mimes of a respectability deflowered a thousand times on African altars in the back aisles of 5 and 10 cent stores. Trucking on and always back to Bahia, aboriginal tracks and time-distances that ran to São Paolo, Manhattan or the Bronx or both, and inexorably back to Salvador.

We had some barley-juice in a bar. Post-Etruscan scene – horses for riding, not for herding, tied up around the square. Dusty Fiats, more like farm machinery than motor-cars, full of neighbours and crates of spring water. I think about Carlos's creative archaeology. I say: 'I've lived among poor people for so long, nothing they do can surprise me. Only judges have to do with poor people as much as me, but I don't feel like a judge. I've lost the emotions based on judging, but not the others. And what hope do we have of repeating those famous colour charts, those autopsies of feeling – James, Lawrence: what of feeling is left for us? A bore to repeat all that, to feel it all again, and in the name of analysis. Can we speak of new emotions? Or do we just confirm, affirm, the old ones?'

Carlos dislikes what he calls my 'didactic style' – a vulture circling, looking for something dead to seize on. 'Bah – there's no poor people here, and anyway, if you're poor you want to get away from them. The awful routine, certainties, little burrowing rounds of poverty. You've no idea.'

I watched a boy inking blue patches on his knees to blend with the holes in his jeans. Carlos yawned: 'There will be no Bahians this year. No one will come over. The austerity programme is succeeding or failing. No one will move.'

'But last year,' I protested, 'the Bahians were everywhere. I met them in New York bars – Luisa was here, living on her expedients: they seemed to have their travels planned for all time.'

'Not this year. Why don't you marry Luisa?'

'How's your fish?' I asked. He was eating it.

'It is disappointed.'

I couldn't marry Luisa. 'I've no money. I look horrible undressed.'

'We Brazilians are very pragmatic. She must be used to both conditions,' he said.

'What is done with passion precludes peeping and prying,' I replied. 'And marriage seems the last concern of a creative archaeologist ... "Creative", I mean.'

And what did he create? I proceeded. 'What, for instance, do you expect to find in tombs?'

'Nothing,' said Carlos.

'So the creative part lies in putting things in?'

'What else? People want continuity. If they can't have everlasting life, at least they want the visible signs of a lasting death, surrounded with some style. History is an arrangement of the past – Creative Archaeology does the same in the concrete – or, rather, the tufa and peperino.

Etruscans are very big in Bahia just now. People buy the pictures, and plan their trip for when the austerity is over. But why not write to Luisa – proposing marriage is something we used to do a lot by letter.' He rolled his shoulders, hummed 'Sambafoxe'.

Secret countries, one world. My friends from Bahia – nicely poised (so I thought, since I could find no way to get there myself) between respectability and the long descent through greyer levels of respectability to the honour of the street – had burst on to my scene. Last year, like a hatch of mayfly, they had circled Rome, and my, Etruscan, cities. My roads, cut twenty metres deep into the rock, my wells, my donkeys, necropolitan complexes. Lakes and sky composed of bands of Chinese white.

I thought of Juliao with his bodyguards. 'You must be a strong man,' I'd said.

'No, on the contrary. That is why I need guards.' Carried with him a smell of notaries' cupboards, of wooden skyscrapers devoured by ants. Hands old gold, though the skin of his face is underbelly yellow – hands dark as if he'd cut them off a sleeping Indian. My fantasy again.

We have finished eating: Carlos asks, 'What are those two arguing about?'

'They are Albanians. They can't import bears to Italy. They have two dancing bears which perform all over Kossovo and Macedonia. Here they can't come. One man wants to go home – the other not.'

'Albanians are driven by clear but non-communicable ideas,' says Carlos with assurance. 'Very impatient with those who don't understand. And the bears?'

'Disenchanted, like your fish.'

Carlos begins to talk about Nicolao, lover perhaps of Luisa, perhaps, by this descent, of me. 'Nicolao has lost his brakes, you might say. His fortunes rise, and he descends faster and faster. He once told me – "I'm the fastest man in the world – hit the end-wall, nothing there. Just all burned up, all energy dispersed, dance of spent molecules. Smudge of rust on some old Buick."'

'Juliao had a Lincoln.'

'Yes, he loved his Lincoln.'

So, stasis this year, no Bahians. But why in my head this idea of triangles, of three-legged visits? Yes, they come to Rome through New York, their touchstone. Carlos says: 'This year the pattern changes. Smells of new servitudes, new spaces. Your friends are in Angola this year. I think I envy them. Starting over.'

I think about this. 'And Luisa?'

'I said your friends. Luisa is not your friend.' What, then? And does this mean she may be here?

Through the trees I can see a silver house: polished with moth fur. Reaching a point in old age where everything comes easy because so deep in memory. Making love, playing the heavy Etruscan lyre, humming the bits that are difficult.

Carlos is laughing at me, at his effect. I say, 'But in Angola – it seems to me sinister, politically.'

'Why, because they're pragmatists? Still a Party man, I see.'

'Yes: the party of the critics, but not of the sceptics. Water through stone. I don't see Juliao and Nico back to their roots, the new world redressing the balance of the old.'

'Well, what do you think of Creative Archaeology, if you think they're crooks?'

'It's a scam. But what do I care? Or you?'

But something wrong. Always with Bahians, there is a mystery, always revealed, always revealing a new mystery – not one of the big ones, neon-filled or capitalised. Perhaps just themselves, the tortuous path they take through life. Not their life, you understand. Other people's lives. Yet, something not right here at all: it's out of scale – canary's eggs on chips, cabbage big as a sow with at its heart one tiny metal snail.

'No,' says Carlos, 'things are not always clear.' I agree.

He continues, 'And the bitch of it is, they don't get any clearer. Even less clear. Too much clutter: too many wandering peoples. Scarcely time to lie down and die. Incredible huskings of half-memories. Africans, Indians, Albanians: all very confused notions about geography, God, what's good to eat. And when we make the compromise required to keep the whole show going – total junk. Everything crossbred with everything else to make the mean.'

I said, 'Your complaint's familiar, but wrong. Only by mixing can we even know what elements are. The myth of origins, the pure sources – it's a scam. Creative Archaeology? I'm happy with my fakes.'

'And yet,' said Carlos paying for us both. 'Some kinds of fake, the personal kind I mean – those make you very edgy. I don't think you like a mystery at all – the idea that miracle and lie are made of the same stuff, that looming above the greatest truth there stands the even bigger lie. Looking for the truth is really living with an endless variety of carefully planned deceptions.'

The cowboys rode off in their Fiats. A cat avoided a big white turkey mincing through the square. 'Talking of Christmases past and their ghosts, I'm afraid my offer of the meal took my last money.' He looks shy and shifty.

I said, 'A rash move to precipitate asking me for a loan. I've nothing. I entrust all my money to banks.'

Carlos did not seem displeased. 'I gave a terrible offence in Crete. It's cost me my job and reputation. But no doubt I shall rise again, if not so soon as the third day.'

'How did it happen?' I asked.

'Creative Archaeology is desperate for recognition and respectability, but we're a touchy, if not a slippery crowd. It was on Crete. A conference. I came late to a session, the president just concluding. An Armenian, from Syracuse, NY. I had come from the beach, wet and sandy. My ill-luck I had on a feathered cap. By worse luck I excused my lateness with "My plane, I fear, was late."'

'A justifiable ellision – no doubt a space not mentioned had filled the gap between your flight and beach.'

'Much worse. The president was struck by a wave of laughter at my appearance, my remark. Stormed out.'

'Why?'

'Later, he said – "A trick in time saves two. But two tricks will save nothing at all."'

'?'

'You see, his thesis was that no Greek would ever contemplate manned flight. If he did, he would choose to fly by night, guided by friendly stars and not seeing the awful expanse of sea. Icarus, then, did not fly: he walked.'

'Or taxied?'

'He walked through the tricky tunnel under the sea. That helped the Cretans with their stunts – abductions and the like. His death – not by the sun, but fire: he was burnt, a sacrifice.'

'And you? A tittling Mercury?'

'Worse, always worse. Aghassian, you see, had discovered the tunnel mouth, carved with winged creatures – hence the link. That led – who knows, in his imagination – back to the mainland. But it was me, the swimmer-flyer, knocked his whole creation on the head – a living Icarus, you see, who'd just flown in. So now Aghassian's ruining me.'

I laughed. 'So much for Icarus. Some walk. Some tunnel.'

'Yes, but what is unpardonable is that one scam artist should scam another while he's on the job.'

'No Carlos, something doesn't fit. I can accept it all but not your feathered hat.'

'But yes. Nico sent it from Angola.'

In a parcel marked 'used clothing'.

We are neck-deep in wild orchids. The new excavations look impressively industrial. There is no one to be seen. Carlos pulls a large packet from his map-case. It smells like the living dead – a leaping, overriding smell, not of death but of triumphant, nasty life. Proudly he shows his catch – purple, saddle-brown, tea-rose, but above all the black, gas-yellow and mute-green of dollars.

I said, 'There must be a million there. But the smell. Unmistakable. And they smear.'

Carlos is hurt. 'Not *smear* – the ink's not set. Set is the word. It will be like this for years.'

'Your problem's solved, then. All you need is a loan from someone till they're set and the smell goes away.'

'No,' says Carlos. 'They're not for spending. They're an instrument. Not a loan either. A name, and a strong-box.'

I understand. 'But not my name, not my strong-box.'

'You haven't understood. They represent an instrument. Nico and Juliao "came into possession of them" – all kinds of currencies. All kinds of mercenary.'

'Let them give them to the government: throw them away.'

'No, no,' Carlos is impatient. 'They would be an embarrassment They would cease to be an instrument.'

'They are an embarrassment, they smell. They stink like crime in heat. They shriek for policemen. If I took them it would be like putting a time bomb in a case indelibly marked with my name. Anyone with any other smelly paper could take them away – my name would cling to them, would become their new smell.'

'But in that way too you would be linked to us. By friendship, by trust.'

'But an instrument for what?' I asked.

'I don't know. No one knows. Not for me, that's certain. But – couldn't you see it as a present from Bahia? Are you so timid, so set?'

'No. Why do you say that? I'm angry most of the time.'

'Are you angry now, with me?' Carlos looks hopeful.

'Of course not. You ask me a favour. I, as a friend, refuse. It happens all the time.'

'You don't trust Nico and Juliao?'

I think. 'I trust them. I don't trust their money.'

Carlos replied that that was the way of money, never a gift nor a liability – an instrument, like a knife. Or a tiger. Some tomb-robbers appear, attracted by the smell. They recognise it. Everyone recognises it. It resembles glue from forbidden fish – the fabulous fish from the emperor's pond whose smell pursues the ingenuous hero till he has atoned: years in a dungeon which pass so quickly in a text, a sentence that takes hardly any time at all.

Carlos puts them away. 'You see, I can't even bury them and find them. Yet they represent a great value, a great danger. A great sacrifice.'

'That sounds rather pretentious. The sacrifice comes from other people, not them.'

'No, no,' says Carlos. It is hard to see if he is disappointed or just wanted to try my reaction. To try again, and again. 'They have their power. They are objects *made*, not found. And so they have a story to which they belong, they seek out passions. Not yours, it seems. Perhaps not mine. But they are a plot waiting for their story.'

I told him, 'Think about it. Think what you can do with them. Remember, the story may already have begun, with us both in it.'

'The story has always begun.'

We are both aware of the heat. Here in Etruria only the insects are enormous: there are no large animals to reduce them to scale. Was it even hotter when the little elephants were indigenous here? Or why did they not take root again? Too much meat going for a walk, perhaps.

'What will you do now, Carlos?'

'What we always do. Return to Bahia.'

'And Luisa? You say she is not my friend.' Not my friend. it's true, I should not have thought to call her that. But what then? And if I trust her, how to trust Carlos who tests me, casts doubts himself?

'You do well to romanticise Luisa. She is very romantic. Underneath the pragmatism for which we are so famous. But I shall see her again before you do. I shall tell her everything.'

'Everything?'

'I shall tell her I passed you the message.'

'About the money? The flying hat?'

'About marriage. After all, it was she who suggested it. And it was she who sent me.'

3   *The Fish in the Ocean*

GOBS OF Saharan rain left tracks of sand. Like traces of squid in manuscript ink. People pleased and worried at how near Africa is. Rain spots like hot-lead splashes, like amoebas. 'Everything is "like" everything else. Everything is "like" something,' I said to Pavel, who didn't seem to understand.

My links with Bahia were frail that summer. Pavel had spent a year there once. Knowing at times the bars by the harbour, at times only the street corners between them. His Bahia seemed like Danzig, or Liverpool.

Pavel was too slight to be a bodyguard or frightener. No threat, he could fix things. But he himself stayed firmly on the bottom of the heap. 'I envy you your passport,' I once said. It was a United Nations one. He made a gesture. 'Useless. They think you're stateless. Keeps you out of jail, but on the move.'

He was nearing fifty, when sleeping rough tells on you. He was seen too often, drinkless, alone at a table, looking out, on one of his seven seas.

Pavel had got his passport in exchange for an even shadier, more compromising one. Issued by the wrong side, wrong kind of eagle with the wrong booty in its claws. Nothing he had done was for the public – nothing freely, that is, for its abstract good. He would not have volunteered, to kill or be killed. In that, he was a pure soul.

He had gathered us a good boil-up of snails. Some of them tasted of peppermint, and their shells reminded me of humbug, but the flesh all looked, and some tasted, like nosepickings. I hoped I couldn't get hepatitis, but it also seemed authentic to eat them all, though I should be beyond or above such thoughts.

Intelligent criminals must hobnob with the thugs they fear. And thugs are – just thugs. Pavel was not so bright, but not a threat either. I envied him – I supposed – for belonging to no one state, for being no one's dog. Or, perhaps, a rabid, ownerless one, expelled from every pack.

You can be too honest for crime – and for other jobs, too. The forged money dogged us like a character disposed of in the drama but who at the end insists on coming back, to decompose. I would gladly have done some deal to get rid of it, but what I had was just its smell. West winds brought its reek, I felt, overlying the imagined perfumes of Bahia. Its lively, corpse-like presence revived Luisa's strange proposal. Made it seem – fishy.

Why marriage? Do people still propose that? To bring Bahia to the breakfast table – had I possessed one. That really would reveal all mysteries, and our treasures. Idea of mystery itself deeply conservative. Just lying there, growing in value, unused. Poor idiots jousting round and getting killed, hoping to enjoy it.

Pavel was a mark of our having gone wrong, of some serious misreading, some conduct skewed. He had, as it were, beached up in Rome to set his own wrongs right. Yet who had wronged him? Was he cause or effect? Who could he talk to? Not some cardinal, full of authority but without power. Some cop at the aliens' office, pumped up with power but disclaiming all authority. And why speak to me? I denied everything. Why Rome? Why Pavel, who might be responsible for his genius, but was scarcely to blame for his being dull – a rather ordinary shipless sailor? Prague safely land-locked away, no nostalgia – another stage on a life of passage. No special significance, just left him with a name. Unremarkable in Bahia – a place like Home, where no big shots were natives. Immigrants making what they thought they'd found – ingenuous narcissism.

'Everything is trying to become style,' I said. 'It's all scheming. The feeling is hidden deep in machination, like goose fat in a roll.'

Many of my friends were painters. They never thought of selling their own works. They sold cheap acrylics, bracelets from Bahia, sometimes a stolen leather jacket. Their canvases accumulated. They could no longer keep them in the cars they slept in, or the friend's apartment, or more often, the bend in the friend's stair. Longing for the adventure, containing sex and food, that would eventually provide space, space for them, paintings, perhaps their dog or cat.

Reasoning no longer quite enough. Not just constant change, defeating the careful prints of memory, addresses, numbers remembered. But things terribly skewed. New faces. A feature here and there replaced by something not quite right – eyebrow a salamander, or a gecko. Effects of miracles, or drugs. Impossible to take quite seriously friend with the false moustache, parents who by diet rejuvenate themselves, promise reincarnation before their death – but not before your own. Knowing too much, but not for anything.

Pavel, on his passport, has another name. So do many of my painter friends. Confusion of signatures with different values. Not quite forgers, but signers certainly. I edge round to the question of forgery, interested only in his own story.

'Sailors never carry guns,' he says. 'So when I carried one, you understand, I hadn't been to sea.'

No diaspora, no war, no inescapable affiliation. No harridan in the background, no circumstance, no sworn enemy. In fact, no one, no first cause at all. Carrying a gun just part of culture. Or sub-culture, even. No intellectual pattern in particular, and so no way of claiming sympathy, of striking chords. But – really no background? That runs against our crowded civilisation, its romanticisms, its even slightly strange self-rejection – if it is real – based on close self-knowledge – eyes like a string of beads, glistening beneath the bed.

'Czechoslovakia is almost certainly part of something else. It is already two parts, two units of that something. But whether its time has been or is to come, I cannot tell you. Anyway, nothing to do with me now. All worn away by travelling,' he said.

Cut into the marble pavement before us was one of Cellini's designs for his *Roma futura*. Mechanical circuses, notables in steam cars, and what looked like billboards advertising films. Complacent prelates watching soldiers drill.

'How did you manage to go to Bahia?' I asked.

'They said I had a comrade there, a mate. And perhaps I did. Perhaps it all did happen, just as they said. I must have lost my calm, or so they said. But really, it was quite the opposite. Angry, yes, but very calm. Where we were living at the time there was a pond, and in it goldfish. Mine they were, preserved – you can imagine – with infinite complication.'

'Hard to relate to fish. Perhaps it's also hard for them to join the world of the senses. They are, perhaps, one of the outer limits. Not really entering into our mythology, except as whales, or even monkeys of the sea, the dolphins, Vassily they are all called – or so they told me in Corfu.' I spoke to carry him along.

He continued, 'It's true, I don't much care for fish. Smoked carp, however, is another matter. And sailors don't eat fish. Perhaps because they eat our comrades. Carp are different, though I believe they are flesh-eaters. But then again, all elements are permeable, they interchange. It's all matter, it's all one.'

I could not restrain myself. 'The passport?'

'Yes,' said Pavel. 'So documents are born. I found my mate one day, shooting at the goldfish. Practising.'

'But the deflection? Surely he must have missed?' Always my technician's, my policeman's, scepticism.

'Some he had killed,' said Pavel. 'So I killed him. In the back of the neck. I had him kneel and say his prayer.'

'You're a compassionate man,' I said.

'Yes, I was. then. But it was long ago. Very long ago. Like being born. And like being born, it is the father of all consequences, but not always a close father.'

Well, yes, perhaps. Like all things long ago, they get bigger and stranger than they were. 'And Bahia?' I asked.

'With a killing, it is the details that linger on, in the mind, too. Like it or not, you become the memory of another, you have that wise old corpse knotted around your neck. Being a sailor is not escaping, it is bowing to your fate. And, of course, it's also true that seamen – I, like all the others, really became a seaman, not a sailor – are scum.' He paused, as if determining to go on into more private areas, more confidential tales. After all, to him what he had done must be a badge, like telling as a blind man how he lost his sight; a priest, how he put on his first dog-collar; the beautiful body how she came to have her face disfigured.

'I found I could learn languages,' he said. 'I speak many. Japanese, and Portuguese, of course, but also Turkish and Malayalam. French and German, naturally, but also some Estonian. And Bahia, you must know, you with your obsession about the place, is where you can use, will need, all these languages, and many, many more. I do not speak about the Africans, nor yet about the Indians. I could go on for hours about communicating with the hinterland. For me, it was enough to speak the languages of the bay itself. All we who had washed up there. Though, of course many prided themselves on being in some way original. But the most original had come from somewhere else. Settling down was always a mark of failure, giving yourself aristocratic airs a sure sign you had a little money – and a great fear of losing it. Going to Rio or São Paolo – that's where the real winners and the losers went. The others – traders, hunters, land-sailors, lawyers – either they couldn't go on, or reckoned they'd lost what was after them. Strolled in from the jungle, jumped ship – using their skins as currency, a kind of history, a document – who knows where they came from? Speaking all languages, then pretending they had lived there for generations – stewing and spicing lizards. Witches' brew: nothing to be proud of.'

He stopped, and I asked, 'The passport?'

'Well, that was mostly politics. Justice is stupid – politics even more so. Justice never forgets, politics never remembers.' And there he stopped.

So many goldfish, so many shots. And so much moral co-responsibility. A mark, they say, of being alive, and being human. Suffering for others, at many removes. And does this weight diminish, with time, with distance, with number, or with unconcern? My Etruscans took two days to cut the throats of three hundred Roman prisoners. But surely I have no responsibility for them? Pavel has paid – I must suppose – his price. And now looks down on those, fresh from genocide in the jungle – opening their restaurants in Bahia, city of the saviour. If God were intelligent, how embarrassed he would be by religion. A major leap forward, to abandon knowledge and stake everything on being intelligent.

In the city there are many churches that open for, perhaps, only one day a year. they have their special devotees. Beneath the appearance of the church, there is often a basilica. And beneath the basilica, there is often a temple or, more probably, the room of some cult – partway between an artifice of paradise and kind of clubroom. When I met Pavel in the city, we used to drink in a wine shop, in a street that seemed long abandoned. The customers were like ourselves, connoisseurs of drinking and themselves. The wine – I must say, mediocre – was served on an alabaster bar. Cavallin, the barman, owner, occupier, would sometimes demonstrate its translucence with a candle. Oil he kept in Ali Baba jars: the oil, dark green, with golden underlights. The wine, alas, with sharp, acid eddies of a green like green apple skins.

All unbelievers, we would sometimes go to the rare churches – sacred perhaps to a local saint, some cult-figure or a corporation, kept going tottering and furtive by some old ambulant priest. And we would poke about the crypt, looking for syncretism, the baths, the hypocausts, surprising drawings. Perhaps, the priest's idea of hell, but really a haven for merchants touched by Africa, or Asia, a little circle of devotion, some resident spirit, and some undemanding friends.

Pavel said, 'The nail-makers' church is open tomorrow.'

Half a dozen of us poked about in the basilica under the nave. Under the basilica there was an early Imperial cult room. The walls were blue, the colour of an Etruscan hell. If there had been water here, it would have been more a font than a pool. On the walls we could see what might have been fish, or might have been cult objects, and sometimes big, round, green and white faces, that could have been reflections of our own over the centuries, everything personal had been removed, but the Christians had not bothered to erase the paintings, which were half threat, half promise of a hell, or element, that was more water and suspension than fire and intimate, personal discomfort.

'It's not bad, if it's hell,' I said.

'Why should it be bad?' asked Pavel. 'It's like being drowned in cold water.'

I said, 'Since death is inevitable, it does seem wrong to see it as connected with punishment – or further punishment than it already is. But this is more a tomb than a club.'

'It's like the hold of a ship, a ship with transparent walls,' said Pavel. 'With wild, anonymous things outside. When you feel space limitless outside, you often make yourself a tiny hole to hold you and your mates. Even if you don't like them much. It concentrates the humanity. And after, when the danger's over, you can't get far enough away.'

We could hear the priest garbling the service above, anxious to get away, no doubt dissatisfied with a small fee. There was little to indicate the nature of the cult below. Two oversized hermaphroditic figures on thrones had a look about them like modern African statues – usually made in Bari or in Genoa, offered for sale at the bus station. Unable to carve human features, the authors put breasts on everyone, as a distinguishing mark. Or was that not in itself a comment ill-informed. and alien to the mysteries – slender and homely – shown here? Someone said, 'They could be a fertility king and queen. They're like that in Chad. And at Nippur.'

I felt we should be able to make more of the pyramids of existence on which we stood. or which dropped away inverted below us. The little room could have accommodated minders, sacrifices, even a crowded orgy. Like so much of the city, it promised a subterranean passage to Africa, to the originals of the emotions, the forces, rather lamely pictured here. The kings, or queens, certainly ruled, and were respected there. And were alive. But when we left, it would again all be in darkness.

Perhaps Pavel was right – a cult for sailors who had made the passage to Africa, perhaps inland, perhaps across the desert. Perhaps making slaves, or being them, or trafficking in some form of being or in taking slaves, acquiring affections, dependencies – properties or feelings perhaps worth killing for. Some mild place for reminiscence, where a golden king and queen were remembered as once appearing, crying 'I want her to be queen,' 'I want to be queen.' And in due course brought to a back room in Bahia, where out front Albanians played poker, pirated tapes were sold.

When we left the church, we felt satisfied. 'Gentlemen's archaeology,' someone called it. Mysteries duly seen and speculated over, not penetrated. How could they be. Dead mysteries, no graver than the ones we all bore. Pavel, the executioner, turning him into an ascetic, haunter of churches, enemy of indulgence. And I, with life apart, life in Bahia, slaves, Indians, a million rivers, an industry of sambas. And in the fields, or buried, maybe, walled up in some tomb – one of the millions – my treasure, worthless save in terms of punishment, or of the links it represented with my own cult, my Bahians.

And Pavel said: 'You know, I know them too, your friends. They wanted me to stand beside you. To protect you.'

'From what?' I asked.

'Perhaps from them. Remember, I am a man who killed his lover.'

4   *Nico: Down the Hole*

I T WAS ONLY later that I heard what might be a true story of Pavel's execution of *his* lover from Bahia. I had called him a compassionate man, and perhaps he was that too, but I could not doubt that he was a passionate one. And that the execution of his lover had been the detonation pushing him into his life of wandering, and of asceticism, but, thankfully, of a moral silence, a refusal, perhaps resting on a weight of remorse, or of some punishment or ostracism endured, which made him totally renounce preaching about himself, or others' conduct.

It may have been Nico who let slip that Pavel was known to many on the Bahia waterfront as much more than 'a sailor', or as he himself deprecatingly put it, a seaman. Sitting in cramped quarters, waiting for storms. Doing the same things in different cities: a paid, not quite outcast, nomad.

Failing to assemble desired parts of reality to make a whole, one is forced increasingly to rely on imaginary props. So, the wet autumn evening in London, an air almost of scirocco, the mixture of sexual expectancy and reassurance as one goes to meet one's latest love – never quite came off. The city is Istanbul, and Armenian neighbours keep a watch on the apartment, with shotguns, from a tree. Or one is in the Giudecca, and details of the view intrude. Or the woman is the wrong one, or has a still more desirable friend, or the occasion is a meeting to vote on a resolution not presented till past midnight, and then lost. So, one is always an anachronism, hermaphrodite, anomaly, in one's most beautiful moments. One is not typical of them, and by defence one thinks they are not typical of you yourself – they ignore aspects of reality that should also be included – history, the collectivity, something more than hedonistic reaction. But then, you are finding fault with reality as well as with yourself. And why not?

Nico, I recall, reasoned like this for hours. Proof of a deep discontent, relation between inside and outside, here and there, me and my relationships – stout refusal to cohere.

'We are your future,' he would say, meaning Brazil, or the people he was knocking about with at the time.

'You are a substantial part of our past,' I said, to annoy.

'No, you're wrong. For one thing, we have "the fathers", the fathers of everyone, the people you call Indians,' he replied.

I said, 'You call them Indians too. And don't try playing the "fathers' card".'

'Money is important, but poor people are either waiting, or else they're outcasts. Everyone has family. And everyone can be someone – look at our music, look at carnival. No rich and poor. Look at the card table. And being part of a nation. Being poor is like being an Indian. You can't climb out of that hole, you are what you are made. But even some Indians make it. And if they don't, they are still, always, the fathers.'

But often I had heard Nico giving quite other explanations. Perhaps sometimes he felt the power of his striving – not for money, but to count. And at others the fear of failing, of sliding back into ancestral nothingness, of being no one, being poor in fact and in spirit. Of being despised by those he knew were just luckier than he, or maybe more skilful, or persistent, or better connected, or more aggressive. Or all these things, in a series of different proportions. Nico was a natural militant without a class, without an organisation, a natural social climber who knew there was no ladder, who, if he could, would make today's boss do tomorrow the dirty work others had to do today. He was constantly in motion, a paradigm of an under-class, feared by the bosses who fear for their heads. But cutting off heads was just one little casual part of what Nico did and might do. And he was gentle, or else he would not have worked so hard.

'I was down the hole,' says Nico. He has told me this many times, differently. He likes me to catch the reference.

I say, 'The story by London. The red fascist.'

He knows I'm annoying him. 'Nonsense. And a most important man for those of us who've been down the hole. The biggest hole you've ever seen, this one, much bigger than the one in Boston. You'd think the whole of Brasilia was built on this hole. We had a shift-boss there. Let's call him Jorge.'

'We always do.'

'You know, when you work in a site, drinking is death. Jorge looked after us when we were drunk. Would put us in little holes, cover us up. Otherwise, you'll break a leg, or fall into the machines – the grinders, we called them. But he was a big mean man.'

'What happened, Nico?'

'They gave us the best pop group in Brazil, down the hole. The best rhythms, the best lyrics. We worked, we strutted, we sambaed like crazy foxes. We were mad, all day and all night, under the lights, the rich smell of sap from the trees, the bright insects running off into the jungle blinking like tail-lights. We were mad, like zombies jumping out of the piano, like live drums: we were high on work and music. It was the best time, a killing time, it was like war, like they say it was before they made generals and gunpowder.'

'Were there no ascetics among you?' I asked.

'There was everyone. From São Paolo, from Recife, from Minas Velhas. There was people who lived on milk, who had been athletes, who had been soldiers, who had been unemployed, who had been criminals. And we worked to one band, one rhythm. We jigged in our sleep, we came to work like a jazzed-up centipede, we went home like so many clapped-out *caixas*, so many drums drummed out but still drumming inside to themselves. They gave us money by the hour, and we threw it away to the same rhythms, it burned and sizzled in our hands, it was like a drug that we burned off, like giving our brains a twist, spinning them in our fingers and watching them twirl off like tops among the animals – and what animals, what insects? Butterflies a metre across, and bright yellow, or white above and blue beneath, or grubs that flowered before our eyes – reared up, a shiny grey like plastic and then slid down, like a spy's kit or a conjuror's, all silk, and flags, and smaller beasts, a row of little tents covered with lacquer eyes, a thousand black men with white beards, and blue beneath. Huge things like elephants, or trees, like cities ready to fall, their roots all hollowed out with other cities, men upside down, but all still busy – massive markets, jazzing along with trading, gesturing, no difference between the men in what they did, but some were black and tall, others grey clay, with orange teeth, chewing and spitting.'

'It sounds terrible.'

'It *was* terrible. A power you've never seen, you can't imagine. All socketed in to that same body juice. And sometimes you saw it all detached, a calm as terrible, suddenly microscopic – as if it was a patch of germs or insects hatching, bursting out, so that you vomited and lay there in the copper soil, your knees drawn up, your guts all knotted, steam in your head, nose full of cheese.'

'And Jorge?'

'The best there was. A giant. He had a.38. He kept the jackals off, the rackets, the women who were sick, the beer they dosed with cobalt. Bad for your heart.'

'You sound like a doctor,' I said.

'That's good,' said Nico. 'You should not understand, but you should marvel, and you should respect. They sang the song:

In every hole
There is a pyramid
Pyramid that dances into splinters
Blue splinters
Frying in the sun –
Feel that sun
You burning splinters

– and we like crazy fools screamed out the words, burrowing down to the earth's centre. They say that the core is burning too, a volcano that will explode and send us shooting off. Like so many red slivers of moon.'

'But there was something wrong,' I prompted him.

'Yes, indeed, there was something wrong. Perhaps it was Jorge, or perhaps he just paid the price.'

Hollow phrases tell us there is a secret behind the panelling. Knock knock.

'I asked Jorge one day: "Where do you go at night, chief?" And he reacted. I meant, did he have a regular woman, did he drink with the other shift-bosses, have his own back-room in a bar, or did he just disappear completely, come back to organise the next shift, protect the guys against their enemies, keep the loansharks off, women and their kids, talk to the cops, take reprisals, keep the work going on, the pay coming in: all that.'

I took up the chorus: 'And he reacted as if you'd accused him of something, being on the wrong side?'

'I've lived my life with Jorge. In jail, in the army, in Angola. And the last Jorge now is Juliao – but this time he's a gentleman, a civilian. He's not full time. Jorge never is a crook. Juliao has, deep down, a bit of a crook in him. I love Juliao, as I love myself. But just as I know my limit, I know Juliao has one. Jorge, in all his forms, has no such limit, and so there's no limit to my love. But this time, yes, with *this* Jorge, something was just wrong, just on the turn, just lightly skewed. He didn't have to tell me anything. I didn't care, in any case, what he did. But I cared that he knew he couldn't be trusted.'

'What did he do then?' I asked.

'He sang.'

It was always a surprise. 'So what if he sang,' I said.

'He sang, and he became somebody else,' said Nice seriously.

'But if he could and wanted to, so what?' I asked.

'In the hole, we were just the dregs. But with Jorge, we were his shift. Not because of him, there are always Jorges, you can see them a mile off. But singing for everyone, when he didn't even need to, for the bosses, for anyone: it's like your woman being on the street.'

'So he had an accident?'

'Yes, he took a trip to the basement.'

'As you called it,' I said.

'Yes.'

And so poor Nico was persecuted, and obscurely went to Angola as Juliao's gopher, his henchman. All nonsense, of course. Nico had become the new Jorge, the pure soul, dancing to the music, perhaps, but not using it to console or corrupt, to bring together opposites, the poison and the river which transported it, empowered it – but might also dilute and waste it. The only thing Nico lacked was money, the only thing he could never have. Or, for himself, want. His will was like the iron-tree, the fabulous tree that blunted iron weapons, turned and flattened bullets.

'Angola,' he went on, 'is like being down the hole again. For months you feel totally defenceless, as if scraps of your flesh had been thrown into a barrel of brine and left to pickle themselves. Then you begin to find protection, friendship, hierarchy. Language is very powerful, the best key, the best defence. And then you see that all the interests are there, even though there seems absolutely nothing to be gained. It's like a poker game on the extreme edge of town, the blood from the last game still drying on the floor. And the weirdest thing there too is the music – in the bush you'll hear a song, a rhythm that could just have come off the radio in Bahia. And you don't know what it means, it's such a fragment, like a broken pot. Or maybe ours is the broken one. And the guy singing just goes silent, won't move. Scared.'

'It must be a good place for being scared,' I say.

'The best.'

He begins to tell me a confused story about saving a woman from a fire. 'But was it a real fire,' I ask.

'You know, everyone has a river, and no river runs the same way, so everyone has different coordinates. Well, this fire lit up five, six rivers, till everyone was forced to look, and run, in the same direction. You know these dance-halls, where often an orchestra comes and stays – right out in the sticks, and can't be bothered to move on, or the truck won't go. And the group will just stay put, put down roots. Some go back to the city, but the others stop, being what they were when they were in motion and become plants by that stretch of river. This woman bewitched the little place. Perhaps she was someone's girl, and that's why she stayed, or was someone's girl in town and didn't want to go back. And usually, with all that water, there are no fires, unless someone starts them. No one moves, ever, unless they want to. And I wanted that woman, but I knew she wouldn't move unless she wanted to – and she didn't want. So she had to be made to move. Just shacks, there were, a mechanic, a hotel for playing cards, blacks waiting for boats, a notary. And someone torched the place. Someone with a city knowledge, of what would burn and cause confusion.'

'But this wasn't Angola,' I said, 'It must be Bahia. And what did you make her do?'

'The two places are not so unlike. Or are so unlike you don't make comparisons. Nothing happens anywhere that might not have happened or be going to happen, in Brazil.'

'So you burnt the town to get this woman to move in your direction. It seems a trivial motive.'

'You're quite right,' says Nico. 'But it was important for everybody concerned. Even when she shook me off when we got back to the city.'

I objected. 'The effects were important, but the motive wasn't. The fire to those not in on the story was quite impersonal.'

Nico smiles. 'It was an immense fire. Bigger than judgement day. People were hopping about like the damned and the saved – lives were burnt down into rubies in a twinkling.' I remembered the hot red eyes of the Christ round Juliao's neck, and thought of two lives, two rubies, running hand in hand through the jungle, behind them the stilted huts toppling into the mud, lizards frantically diving.

He drinks his drink. It is the colour of old bananas, or of black-brown fingers round the glass, coming clear as he finishes it, looks round for another.

He says, 'And you are wrong. A fire is never impersonal. It is always *your* fire, if it's after you. It's the most personal monster there is. It has its name, and it has your name, and you never forget it, and it never forgets you, and it follows you far beyond the world's end, it hangs itself round your neck and it burns for ever.'

Nico is wild, is running. It is a headlong advance that drives you to follow, not from trust but from fear, yet it is not from fear – why should it be – that I ask, 'It was Luisa?'

'Yes, it was Luisa.'

Later, I say to Nico, 'That adventure was about you, but it started off being about Pavel.'

He looked uninterested. 'Yes, it was just that Pavel made a fuss about the boy, a terrible fuss. A fuss that fussed the whole of Bahia. And then he killed him. Why, I don't know. No one that I know was interested in the boy. No one was interested that Pavel had polished him off. When you look at him, do you think Pavel is still that interested?'

'And the goldfish?' I asked.

'What goldfish?'

When I had explained, Nico said, 'He's got goldfish in the head. That's where the goldfish are.' And he added wisely, 'Goldfish in the head.'

5   *Luisa: Home Thoughts from Home*

RELATIONSHIPS *are so sticky. Interminably viscous. And, after all, why does one try to free oneself of them? Completely. Relentless male voices on the radio. Modulated for every mood, except for selling food. They're moving even into drink, pouring it themselves at home. In Rome, even with* him, *I feel freer. Bahian voices, trapped in their culture, or bringing some strange one with them. Even he has a personality like a tree's roots. Objectively, no one is too likeable, but for we* subjects *– my God, still more stickiness. And we spin webs, try to stun him, tie him up, make him a tiny slave, we tiny slaves. Ants in Bahia, pretending we're really from Recife. Recife, indeed!*

But in Rome I do feel free. Alone – but never alone, a woman is never alone, or if she is she knows it's the end – I feel more precious, more charged with precious things. More vulnerable, more dangerous. Perhaps a prisoner of myth, too, but then that is the price of being with others – civilisation.

I remember in Naples seeing a boy of thirteen selling cobs of maize on the street. And no doubt 'doing' other things. He was an only son, his parents worked a bit. I said, 'In Bahia, he would be in school.' They said, yes, there is something wrong with our politics. 'No,' I said, 'with your culture.' We don't know if we'll ever get out of our hole. But we try, we all try, sometimes exaggeratedly. And of course, you're being rich and trivial attracts us. That too is civilisation.

I suggested marriage, a pact, to him. Against the world, but in it. But he'll refuse, resist being part of our poor empire. Caught in his old fears, his old autonomies – a province of one. In the end he sees it all just as a business: being married, being together, being part of a network. For him, in the end, it's all just contracts. He's squeezed all the adventure out, in the name of humanity.

Anyway, we all speak with cracked tongues. When music was one of my expedients, I worked with a group called Vox Pop. In Rome, and perhaps with my lover in Rome, it is a buried pop. So many peoples, struggling up from the catacombs. They always said we excelled in 'poverty and banality of expression'. Perhaps we diluted the good stuff. They didn't see pop was just a project like others – and not for making money, but for being conscious of it: seeing how poverty of means, poverty of emotion, even that could make money: never enough, never for what we wanted.

That is why Rome is so important a part, a stage, of our project, of my project, and then Juliao's, and Nico's, and the others. All the misshapen pieces to be fitted together.

If politics was the art of compromise, pop was its science. I couldn't face being the new Brazilian woman. Our teachers used to talk about African deities, matriarchy. I told them, every teatime in our street is full of that. Horrible old women, asking you in for an excuse to snip off some pubic hair. What stuff they put in your cakes, and what spells to keep their husbands' ghosts away: I told them – the teachers – "Believe me, leave that stuff about Africa alone. It will land you a hundred years back, and at best you'll all get to be fascists." Quite uncritical, quite unintelligent, they were. 'I don't want to be a woman,' I said. 'I am one. I want to be something more. If I use these old tribal figures, I want to use them in my songs, along with the Greek porn newsagent and the billiard saloon with the new orange tables – I don't want to believe in them, justify them.' And they said I had to fight, but as a woman. So I fought, but not as a woman. Yes, I suppose first of all I fought against them – and as we said, sex is incidental.

Yes, often very incidental. And there is a part of me that doesn't want to be Grace Jones. There is a part of me that hates Grace Jones, that would hate myself if I were Grace Jones. Just as there is a part of me – or perhaps it is the whole of me – that wants to walk down the Avenue of the Liberator with two jaguars – naturally, not on leashes – and to be Jenny the Pirate. But not on the stage, and not singing a little song.

And there is in me something that hates all forms of our nationalism, left or right, all this putting together incongruous and unmixable bits and pieces: and calling this miserable, garish kitsch a country, a nation. Like calling currants and cherries a plum cake. This plumcake kitsch we knew all about – and we called it popular music. And instead of being bought and sold and used like saucepans and bottles of whisky, it ended up in frames – all part of a meretricious babble of tongues. Mr Galsworthy and Mr Amado, that elegant mixture of tongues and voices. But, how do you subvert plumcake? And the old witches brewing tea from monkeys' foreskins?

Did our lyrics catch that knowing bourgeois voice and send it back bewitched, imploding, eaten up with jazz-ends as if termites had been at it? I don't think so. We were Disney, street boys and rude, but in the end, just good old uncle Walt, down on the unions and hot on good tunes and lots of schmalz. Strumming our guitars, thinking of Paris, setting up our tribal drums and rattles under the spots. Who are you trying to kid, Mr Galsworthy? And us?

The people, yes: and no. As an audience, they never impressed me. And as actors in their own right – even less. Nico once said to me, 'Democracy is consulting people who are wasting their lives.' And I said, 'If they didn't waste their own, they would have them wasted anyway.' I know I could put it another way to make myself more liked. But singing gives you a low opinion of your public. All the tricks, and all the work you put in – to make a little thread of all, or else a big, orange roaring. Then, it's all gone. It's all connivance: they want to cry or to applaud. And there you are, in tights or dinner jacket – or, indeed, both. Performing, you live on the edge: you ride on the edge, a line of brightness moving through, before and after there is nothing.

Rome appeals to me – the biggest theatre in the world, no distinction between indoors and outdoors, underground and in the air. It's all worked space, smells like a workshop, artisans are cobbling up the sets, the costumes, stage machinery – choruses of everyone from everywhere – devils rising and falling through trapdoors, the boxes full of popes and presidents. And my lover? Impresario. Impresario we can't do without – not the claque, but more loyal, more reliable, brighter, than any claque. If there is a force, an explanation of that travelling line, maybe it's him – part the tormentor, part the Hercules.

Not to act any more, but to perform – yes. To go on tour. To be the centre, black star stealing the light, burying light. Burying light in the black lake and every night bringing up a netful.

Get together some decent musicians, guys who can at last play together. You don't have to be good to play with me, I said, you just have to make me sound good. Anyway, I am good, I do sound good. Quite indifferent to trumpeting lovers, drummer with a clip-on beard. Play what I tell you. But the centre – yes. Look for the centre. That's where I am.

In Bahia, we only judge individuals. And we judge them hard, even if the sentences are tolerant. But the nuns – the nuns in São Paolo – judge by time. In very short periods: and the people are like the stamps they give you in catechism classes. Rich man, beggerman, policeman, thief. Or all in one. Their hatred is contained in what they do today, not what someone may do tomorrow. They don't ask what can become of all this cruelty. Nico says, it is to be mastered like anything else. But I feel it as a living creature, like those creatures they say lie under the whole of Brazil, whose sweat is the rivers, whose dirt is the fields, whose hair the forests and whose shit is the minerals. We played once to an audience of miners – under a shroud of mud they had brown overalls, and under those there were brown men. Everyone, all over the world, washes for a concert, a fiesta. They laughed, and said, 'The water's brown.' Brazil, for the three times brown.

And yet they had brown wives, brown children, they lived in brown huts and ate brown food. Only their sky was blue, and the insides of their mouths. They didn't open them much in case the brown got in.

Whole awful continent a mess – the US upstairs part, where the masters and servants live: 'I have seen the future and it drives you mad.' Best thing there is the bacon, because they feed the hogs so well. Brazil itches on me like an eczema. Maddening politeness of Bahia, crazy company of salesmen and witch doctors. And New York, where we go to talk about Bahia. And Juliao does his business by the East River. A cardboard box factory? Shoe liners? Importing kilims? or Peruvian slaves? At least it's something legal.

So, not Rome but Etruria – too dull and silent for Italians. Strange people, my lover's neighbours – last resistance against Italy. Dogs riding pillion on the donkeys through the bamboo groves. A way to avoid cities, and public works? But no – all that engineering, the waterworks, the sunken roads – all a quarry. Now, quite unambitious. Waiting again to be pillaged, partially learn new languages.

6 *Juliao and His Collateral Campaign*

A ND YOU,' Juliao asked me. 'Where are you at
now?'
'Trying to sort out a Marxism no one understood
from a communism no one wanted, it seems.'

'That could be a long job.'

'Yes,' I said. 'I think so too.'

'Well,' said Juliao. 'What do you advocate? What is
your moral charge now?'

Indeed, advocacy there must be, but what principles?
Abandon the principles and stay loyal to the people? It
seems silly to think the moral charge is exhausted because
you have somewhat burned your fingers on it. And, after all,
there was always the complexity, moral or not, which made
cynicism come easily. But – after all – these are just alibis
for keeping on, pushing the same closed door.

'Or at least, what do you think of our plan?' asked
Juliao.

'In some ways it attracts me, but in others it seems naive,
and above all empty. It meets the need for action and for
purity – but it's contentless, generic. A humble kind of
official busy-bodying. I think to save their souls, our souls,
people must speak out, be left outside, not as a formula but
because things are like that.'

'Sheer, random individualism,' said Juliao. 'You're
talking about a league of academics. Criticism is one of
their privileges. So is reading books. But they may not do
much of either. And being privileged makes them
vulnerable on one side, and arrogant on the other. And you

know that for every one who makes a funny monster there are hundreds selling demijohns of poison.'

But how to trust them? How to trust myself. Herzen spoke of the courage required to leave the ancestral mansions to go and construct uninhabitable hovels. But his was a choice between comfort and uncomfortable precariousness, not between precariousness and jail.

Juliao explains the project expansively. 'In the past, there have been consultants – who in the end have gone away in failure, or concentrated their ideas in little schemes, profitable for them and their bosses; or empires, or bankers, or arms dealers. Or there have been people who came and worked, became rich and retired; or worked, became poor, and were ridiculed. We, in keeping with the globalisation of enterprise, propose instead to insert a party: the party of the critics. We shall live in the country involved and, using our best principles, constructively but constantly act as critics of everything that exists.'

'It's absurd,' I said, feebly. 'What principles? what criteria? It's arbitrary, self-defeating and self-contradictory. And besides, you need money.'

'We have begun to get the money. I, Juliao, have begun to get the money.'

'But that money is false. And it smells.'

He was uncomfortable. 'It may yet turn out to be a means of exchange. What is a critical idea worth anyway? What do you have to back it?'

He explained further: voices of dissent, the separation of critique and construct. Only a Brazilian far from home could have proposed such an idea.

I said, 'But critical ideas are out of fashion.'

'Yes, now you have hit on a weak point.'

'And Luisa,' I asked, having scored a critical point which may have served, after all, as justification for the scheme.

'When Luisa says she feels freer, it means facing easier problems. In Bahia she is unable to sing, even unable to speak. She's organic there, and doesn't like it.'

'But she is behind the idea? Or is that my mistake?'

Juliao concentrated. 'She is sceptical. But she wants to do something, and for her, establishing the Roman pole is a satisfaction. I refer, of course, to Rome for its geography, not its rituals.'

Juliao labours over the abstracts.

He continues: 'And there is, of course, for her, yourself. A physical presence is of importance to her. She thinks highly of you.'

I am unsettled. 'But you are describing an adventure, and with grown-ups involved we fall into the world of dangerous pleasures: drugs, spies, foundations of a supposedly charitable nature.'

Juliao at last smiles. 'That is why you must trust us. As we have from the beginning trusted you. Your openness of judgement; undoubted intellect, even if – so far – it has lacked a focus, has dwelled too much on buried and ambiguous peoples, like Etruscans.'

'But, Juliao, you must see that the patterns are not just empty forms: the tracks, the voices, carvings, compositions, the patterns you find in people, human arrangements – these are not plastic, random. They are reality. All you can do is alter your viewpoint, your distance. I know where reality is, and I must be part of reality for you. You can't invent a future for me, move all the lines and colours about.'

'But certainly we can,' Juliao is playing with a beetle in the shape of a lump of brownish jade. I get his point. 'We can *offer* you something immense. Humanly – our support.

For yourself – new life. A world to be built, designed, conceived, imagined.'

'How can this end?' I thought.

'If you think, "How will this end?" said Juliao, 'it is better not to start. The proposal is not to give you some religious rebirth, where the past is a mysterious mistake and the future is planned. You are being given the chance of stepping out of the frame, out of preconceptions, out of limitations of your individual self – but into a context of action, of usefulness, not contemplation.'

'On the contrary,' I said, 'it seems I am being offered the choice of entering *your* story, of becoming a character in your plots, with an end – whether at this moment it has been contrived or is still indeterminate or guessed at. I am asked to become part of your design.'

'No,' says Juliao. 'You are being invited to leave your own design, which is arid, whose limits you know so well, and for which you too are responsible. I remember the story of a girl who volunteered to leave Leningrad to work with the peasants in Central Asia. To her friends it was an exile of the soul, the end of feeling. To her, every morning, seeing the apricot trees, seeing the mist rising from the horizon – every morning was like the first. A sacrifice which was not a loss of everything, but just an exercise of the will. Who wanted to go shopping, to discuss poetry, sit in offices, tramp from one history lesson to the next? It was not important. That was a paper life, swamped with tons of paper, life sitting before the typewriter – reports, articles, orders, plays – all the same. A pedantic plodding life.'

'But could I do it? And in any case, this is not the use of critical intellect, but of another kind of will.'

Juliao is vindicated. 'Exactly. The intellect has been used for invention. But it has refined itself so that it only recognises and responds to the rustling of papers, to its own droppings. The contemplative intellect, and all *that* criticism has lost contact with the exercise of will.'

'I heard all that a hundred years ago,' I say, though really I am relieved to see a familiar landmark in a desert of challenges.

Juliao replies: 'Yes, it is a banal statement. But deny your will to live, not to think passively, and you will implode, as if you had denied your will to sneeze: or breathe.'

Convention gave me only one line, to say: 'When do I start?'

7   *A Lesson in Political Economy*

JULIAO instructed me: 'Capitalism represented the disorder which sweeps away and survives a previous order. In turn, it becomes an order. In all probability it will be swept away in disorder. In Brazil we have many orders, many fragments of ancient orders, but these cannot be stuck together – the forest, the river, the coast, the plain. I, personally, enjoy disorder. I'm a revolutionary, but also an anarchist. So, I made some money with capitalism, which is, if you like, just a form of criminality – except that crime is more personal, more human. With criminals, you recognise something that goes back to the roots, that ends in a straight splitting of skulls, a reconciliation of families.

'Disorderly capitalism soon outgrows that phase. It becomes something like a war between nations, where you deploy masses of men in uniform you never know – common soldiers without boots, officered by gourmets. And from this war comes order, comes discipline, hierarchy. Or a frightful defeat – or both. But let us suppose the best: a truce, a series of standing armies. Making the career, dying with your boots on. Disorder is also death, the wish for death. Our bodies are bound to rhythm, order. That's why I want to break that chain, of order-disorder.'

I said, 'I seem to have heard this before.'

8   *A Trace of General Winter*

I SEE JULIAO'S thoughts breaking like smog on the cliffs of Manhattan. He looks tired, even ordinary. He looks like a guard at a boot factory in Gary, Indiana. Who has seen the name Bahia in a travel agents and has overlaid it with an image of grass skirts. Or perhaps that is the syncretism of the agency itself. He has ordered a water ice, and played with it while it fades away. He has a tiny ornament brought with him, and he is fiddling with it. I ask, 'What's that? A plastic penguin?'

'No, a salamander.'

He is disappointed in me. He is saddened by his own presence, by his distance from Africa, by the drabness of his suit. In his breast pocket I see two pens and a torn packet of Happydent.

I reminded him, 'Lenin's trousers were too long when he went back to Russia in 1917.' Juliao looks surprised, then happy. He says, 'You're right. I'll go back to the inelegant style. No more designer fatigues.' I am oppressed by the trivialness of our ambitions, of our journeys from one side of the tide to the other. The waiter takes away the saucer and the salamander: the bar is closed. It is hot, but we are sweating so much it feels cold. There is something wrong with Juliao's story – but there is something wrong with everything here – the cars all seem to have been repainted after being stolen, the bottles all hold liquids of the wrong colours. Only the undrinkable purple Bols has not been switched – to con us everything is in its place.

Juliao relieves me by saying, 'I think we shall all go to jail.'

'Yes, I think so too,' I reply. The world is ending very quickly as if its composer has reached the bottom of his last page of manuscript paper. Tables being piled; the last dry nordic chords. We shall be taken away.

Juliao whispers, 'But you must help us, for Luisa.'

Now we are outside, and there is new life. I object: 'Luisa is again in Bahia. The place is booming, computers have transformed the samba schools, Brazilian debts are the world vacuum in which no plucked goose's feather falls.'

Juliao says gloomily, 'Luisa should arrive in a few days. But you get no pleasure from her. Only from seeing a piece of the puzzle move. You're cold fish.' Does he perhaps mean both of us?

9 *Aghassian*

I RAN OUT to shoo away some possible visitors. Aghassian was used to such reactions. He had acquired a mean dog for the back of his rented truck. It stood in the shell as victor of a decisive battle. I was relieved. Aghassian did not visit, he went on expeditions. 'You've made peace with Carlos, then,' I said. And he: 'Carlos is having trouble with some sheep on his trailbike.' Carlos had come too.

Unusually, the village children are attracted to adults: I almost say 'unaccountably'. Perhaps because they have few toys, and footballs often gain lustre by being played with by grownups. Aghassian, however, looked at the plastic balls as though they were fungi. 'Brown cats in pots are sad,' he said. He reduced my environment to eccentricity in an instant, without losing his grip on his own. 'My cats like being close to the flowers,' I said. 'Right – touch of NY there – but *hanging* pots?' he says.

Aghassian told us, as he must often have told Carlos before. 'I can't stand the digging kind of archaeology. I like to fly and snap. Keep my aerial distance. Interpretation's my strong point. Learnt it on spy planes.'

We went inside. I could feel myself becoming the subject of Aghassian's acrid stories, himself unconcerned at being caricatured, and indeed seeming to regard that as a desirable aspect of personality. He quizzed me on local archaeological pundits: 'Voss, Canguilhem, and of course the Danes.'

'Ah yes,' I said. 'The Danes.'

'Pushed measurement to the limit,' said Aghassian. 'I admire them for that. If an area *can* hold x tombs, assume it does and start looking for them. A masterly statement of the maximalist case.'

'Yes, of course. Yes.'

Aghassian continued: 'Aerial photography is essential in Africa because of the flat-level profiling – that and the whole question of time-plan foreshortening.'

'Yes, yes, of course.'

Carlos looks desperate, comments on a hedge of tomatoes ripening. Aghassian heads him off. 'Yes, green to red is an odd transition, though often found in nature. Green to red through blue and purple is a shorter trip wavewise. You'd ripen quicker by that route. You'd have to bombard them with shorter waves, of course.'

We, Carlos and I, probably look miserable.

Aghassian sheers off. 'Want to put my creative archaeologists on the ethical dimension,' he says. 'Take Albany, for example. Suppose it's flattened by a bomb blast. What does that tell us about human relations? I mean, the quality of life there. The singles bars, the places where the gays hang out. And family life, the churches, the ethnic halls.'

'All from a safe height,' I add waspishly, and regret it.

'That,' Aghassian continues, 'is what people need to get from us. How did the vanished peoples take their responsibilities, their couplings and uncouplings, their ties, their hedonism, their baths and brothels? That's the title, by the way, for our next conference. "Baths and brothels." How about human relations in this part of Etruria?'

'Oddly enough,' I reply, 'I never thought that was other than pure speculation. Talking that way about the private makes it part of the public domain, and, democratically, everyone's say is worth anyone else's. Up to a point. It's the Aristotle problem – what is most authentic is what is most typical: what is most intimately specific is recognisable only as exemplary of its type. That's why some people like to read and write novels: we think we're getting something absolutely true and genuine because the characters don't exist. But in order that they might exist, they must fit patterns already broadly familiar to us.'

Aghassian turns playful. 'Cummahn. I hear your Luisa's a special bit of stuff. Belting out the old torch-songs. And everyone knows Brazilians have a sexual continuum twice the length of North Americans. Yes, indeed. We've all been moths to her flame, believe me.' He adds, 'In our time, of course.'

It is like waiting for people to emerge from some dark digging somewhere. All blanched and blinking, indistinguishable. They see and identify you, but they themselves are all the same, same shorts, sundresses, stretches of unoccupied flesh.

'Great people,' he continues. 'Africans. My own people, I believe, came from those parts, losing, as is clear, the characteristic pigmentation on the way. Much in common with the copts, and at once by nature both sectarian and traditionalist.'

I add, 'Conservationists too, if we are to believe the Noah story, and presume he would have let out a sea anchor so as not to land too far from home.' My error, of course.

'Well, as you know, we Armenians have no right to claim the Noah myth. The idea of a high mountain is one rationale. But a low mountain, knoll in a desert land, fits just as well. In short, I'd say that Noah landed in an oasis.'

And, indeed, why not try again: 'Carlos seems to have lost position to your dog – does he have some characteristic that stops him sitting down?' The dog had never put its front paws to the ground, whereas Carlos had sat disconsolately and in silence.

Aghassian kicked playfully at the dog. 'Mihailovitch? Great company. Bounding energy. Take him home – a good yard dog. Carlos, on the other hand – what shall we do with you?'

Stirred to react, Carlos said, 'Our friends in Africa are sending us more maps. It seems some kind of aerial survey has a lot of backing.'

Well, yes, even I can see it would, especially under the banner of Aghassian's scam archaeology. But is he really part of us, our filmy network that might turn back into seaweed or refractions in a mermaid's eye if too hard tested?

But Aghassian is steaming ahead into Luisa. 'Forgive me if I say this, but all the women in Brazil, and for me Brazil means just Bahia, are by nature queens. Their trouble is, they're used to slave empires – free men excite and trouble them. In both cases, you see, *they're* free to do what they like with *them*. Their authority is as great with free men as with slaves – even more so. But something is changed, unclearly.'

'Like Barbarella,' I put in.

'Luisa is a classic case. Born to command, at all costs – especially to others. But what the hell do you tell free men to do? Love you? But love supposes reciprocity, sharing of powers. And a queen's powers can't be shared, or she loses the chrism. Our realm of freedom gives us only love, love is the only coin of symbolic exchange. But it's just a coin. It's not obedience, loyalty. It's worth the same anywhere. Typical would be my dealings with Mihailovitch. And, wow, Luisa has a body. A body fit for a queen.' He stares at me. 'Not many of us could match that.'

I ask Carlos, 'Did our friends send anything but maps', thinking of his flyer's hat and not of money. Carlos looks guilty. 'Yes, they sent a lexicon. Words they think we might hear in Bahia – but the transliteration's difficult.'

First a magic hat, and now a list of incantations – times are hard. But Aghassian has picked up the thread of this labyrinth as well. 'A universal language? Well, why not. The commerce of slaves is probably the oldest form. Beneath all our civilised tongues there'd lie – why not – not deep structures but a slave argot, as old as Africa. Beneath the free religions, the twists of noir and scraps of life taken as consolation, memories of tribal homes. The whole superstructure based on the dreams of unfree peoples. Turned back on them, abstracted: the redeemer of the free is thus a gutted slave, his message passing, meaningless now, to the slave dealers, a consolation, a hope of heaven and deliverance even after all the hard work's been given over to the skivvies. Yes, I like the concept. Very neat.'

'Lenin called it skinning the ox twice,' I said. Carlos twitches at the name. Is this really the hero striding from the sea, from firmament into convention room, silencing the microphone and the simultaneous translation?

There is a sudden confusion in the house. I say, 'I think my cats want to use your chairs.' Mihailovitch prances fussily. We all finish the encounter standing, except the cats.

Aghassian says, 'Look, I've got so much to take back to Syracuse. Lots of contacts, lots of fresh ideas. I'll let you all know. Especially you,' not too friendly, to Carlos.

The children have twisted Aghassian's truck, but deftly he puts it back in shape. No mean magician himself. Screams off, the dog's tail flying like a lancer's banner.

Carlos says goodbye. 'Well, you blew that interview all right.'

'So did Aghassian.'

'Yes, maybe. But he could have been our paymaster.' Carlos looks exhausted.

'But you could see he's CIA. Or couldn't you? They're the only ones who know so much. Don't you remember: "Speaking of the austral cone, Angola's the periphery or, if you prefer, the gateway to another domain. What turns it from periphery to something else? Why, the nature of the other side, of course. What lies beyond, in what was outer darkness? And the lateral belt, just north of Capricorn? A pretty empty area of the world, unless you count the water."'

'I don't remember,' said Carlos. 'I thought he was talking about Noah.'

'Perhaps he was,' I say, 'about conservation.'

'And anyway,' Carlos continues, 'the CIA will work down there for the duration. We shall have to come to some agreement – or, rather, some agreements, with theirs and ours and others still.'

'And Luisa,' I ask. 'Does she, or did she know he's CIA, or just think he's a scam artist?'

Carlos at last puts on his winged hat. 'I must be off. Well, you know, at one time in Brazil Americans could open every door. And Aghassian knows everyone.'

'And everything?' I ask. 'And about the money?'
'No, if he knows, it's not from us. The only thing – is if Luisa tells him. For some purpose or some weakness of her own.'

He is astride his trailbike. 'Or else,' he goes on, 'perhaps to help you out. Make life easier for you,' his words but not his meaning whine off.

10 *My Letter to Luisa*

'**W**HILE *I have, I suppose, been waiting for you, a series of people from all over have come making proposals and bearing messages that may be from you. I have in the end an impression that you are too diffident to show your own (I almost say, your own real) face. But you were never afraid of that.*

'*So, I accept your proposal of marriage. It would be amusing to do so, and will be amusing in its development. It is a big step you have made for me, and a big step you have made towards me. They say that 'it is quite common in Bahia for women to do this', but I do not think this can be true, and in any case it is quite irrelevant for those involved. However, what is suggested is suggested in a public way, and so must fit some public expectations – perhaps this letter is a way of meeting some of them.*

'*Otherwise – what the hell is going on? I am stunk out of my province with funny money. You are described as a queen and-or the whore of Babylon. There is some operative from the CIA who speaks knowingly about you and probably has aerial photos to prove it.*

'*In such heady discussion of goddesses and queens, I'm happy to be a gruff captain from the steppes, but rising to captain is itself quite a feat, and deserves recognition. I should think in a modern marriage, content counts more than form. Or, again, it may not. It may be quite the reverse. However, if plane tickets are required – and frankly, I should prefer to remain here – let me know, and I shall make the arrangements. Perhaps you could send some (genuine) cash too, as my expedients have been working badly.*

'*Against my will, and ever since those NY bars, I am forced to rely on Nico and Juliao. But I must know who is at the centre of the project. Is it you? And who am I – the Man Without Qualities? Two people determined to be at the centre of their own lives can have a relationship, but it is disturbing if one of them is uncertain where this centrality lies.*

I'm not raising – at least directly – questions of power, just of perspective.'

And so on.

Re-reading the letter, and imagining it travelling to Bahia, stopping for frequent rests and sea-changes in post-offices and lying in bonded wharves, it seems pompous and eccentric. It could have been written by a nonagenarian Harpagon with gold under the bed disturbing activities on it. I had little to give and nothing to lose.

I could have added – '*The private aspect is OK. The public one does, anachronistically, worry me. Believe me, it could all go badly, and end worse. The puzzle was not after all very hard. You combine tourism with archaeology – building an international network and some spurious respectability on archaeology, with its small but ultimately luxurious projects. And you associate all this digging and flying with tourism from Brazil, and the cultural affinities, the roots, that in some, undoubted, various ways exist between them. You thus have your "critical" projects of exploration resting on new links, new systems, of commerce and ideology.'*

Where was the danger? The Brazilians would push, the Angolans yield or resist according to mood or interest. We should have first the illusions of starting a grandiose design, and later a long siege by bankruptcy. Debts first to Brazilians, then to Italians, Americans, disappointed by creative archaeology. Simply the normal grinding of commerce, the well-known ethical delights of operating in the world market. Going under or being taken over. I was unenthusiastic. But in what sense was this to be avoided, save as an expedient more desperate, more tedious, more inflated, than any of my own?

None of us wanted to do *this*: we all wanted to do, to accomplish for ourselves, something else. That too, after all, the soul of commerce. But the mixture of desperate and incompetent people engaged in a grandiose political project – since that is how we saw it, even if disguised as a cultural one – had already attracted Aghassian. One, perhaps many, corpses we already had: the pale coffin-lined dollars with bright sprinklings of gangrene, lying hidden, hidden by their mercenary comrades, buddies of currencies we could not decipher. And which could have been genuine.

In any case, Luisa didn't answer. Perhaps she had not had the letter. It would not have worried me.

But, instead, she comes.

'No magic here, just attenuation,' she said.

We were watching the army helicopters practise landing behind the dark-age castle. Now, just a shell of blackish titanic rocks, it kept its colour throughout the day, at dusk lightening a little to blue, then grey. The tombs of the necropolis, rising the height of the valley, started pink at dawn, then in the sun went down to grey. In the late afternoon, the little lights of ice-plants receded, and the whole bulbous complex went orange. Samphire and tormented baby oaks seem to shoot out of the crevices and blind squinches on the façades.

If you had nothing more grandiose to do, you could spend the day here, watching the history of colour, or of decor. Etruscans would probably have weeded, cut back the tree cover. Luisa was right. In these places there was no mystery, just places of death designed to fade, without regret or bitterness. Rock hollowed out to be returned to rock, a little honeycombing known only to family, soon to be dead themselves, interred by other worker bees, or else roasted in pots and put in niches.

The helicopters buzzed and bumped. I said, 'In between the dead and the soldiers, my neighbours will pass away in ten years. Already they're capering to new rhythms. I think this part of my story is ending. Must get closer to the centre – or just far enough away to get the sense of movement.'

Luisa says 'There's no centre, just grids of energy. And here the grid's just pencilled in. I like places and people in flux, rivers when they take off as if called, the trumpet's line disappearing off the page, up the chimney, with the birds into the mountains.'

The manoeuvres are coming to an end, trucks are coming to pick up the pieces, take the soldiers home for another try tomorrow.

It seems we who do not dance to necessity slide in and out of the narrative mode. We live at times quite fragmentarily with other characters. An old man silent at the end of the street fills part of the need for silence. Fortunately, we never follow him home, listen to his crazy singing to his grandchildren, boring everyone with sea-tales. Then people start to interlink: they hurry together, flow, make a current and draw us along, making us wonder who is in control. Did we fall into all this movement, or are we deftly navigating? I say, 'My neighbours are bound by iron rules of custom. They discuss them all the time. And yet they live all ways, as they can and as they must. In Bahia too they must do the same even more. The difference is that the steps, the divisions, are sharper. If you slip, it's as noisy as falling downstairs and as painful. To climb the hierarchy, you must put in a huge effort and believe in it all.'

'Yes,' says Luisa, 'The carnival that once attracted you makes no sense unless there are those staircases. But many, many of them. Going, quite indifferently, both ways. Perhaps, then, I'm just lazy – don't want to climb or fall.'

'It's an aesthetic idleness. You want to contemplate and then dominate effortlessly, building a whole new elevator for one.'

Luisa understands: 'You think we're wrong to hustle along in the project – or Juliao's version of it? We should lift ourselves up, throw ourselves about, pile ourselves up, like Chinese acrobats?'

'I don't know,' I say. 'At the moment, we belong together. We fill different needs in a phase of narrative, of movement. But the lines are in harmony. If we don't necessarily make beautiful music together, at least there's a succession of stirring chords.' It's good that Luisa does not want some concrete compliment instead of endless metaphor. Still, by now she must know her hair is this way, her skin fits so and so, and less so here: she doesn't need applause for smiling, looking, speaking.

We scramble out of the valley. The first explorers, over a century ago, were led here by people they found hanging about the inns. So, they were places never really lost – just neglected, even concealed. These English discoverers brought back their sketches, tales of combat with sheepdogs and malaria, measurements and underestimates of what was here. What, though, did they really bring back, from this strange, African Lazio? No Victoria Falls, no headwork, no music, no tribal masks: not even Catholicism, already soundly rooted out, at least for a time, in explorers' England. Proof of backwardness, of 'good fellows, with Etruscan features'.

Luisa breaks in. 'I must tell you, I'm here not just casually, but because I want to be. Nico asked me to go to Africa with him, and so did Juliao, in his way. We've gone a distance along these roads together, and I said I'd stay with you – but not to pretend we don't have our autonomy.'

I smile. 'I know. When I last saw him, Nico told me he would ask.'

11   *More '49-ers*

L UISA AND I went with Pavel on another exploration.
'Why this passion for holes in the ground?' she
asked. 'Why don't you ever go up?'

'A fair question,' I said. 'It's reassuring when history is
under your feet and you only need to surface to be normal
again.'

Pavel is looking old: not ill, just old. He says, 'We're
looking for the caves the defenders of the Roman Republic
hid in when the papal troops were after them.' I have asked
Luisa if she knows him: 'I know the type,' she says,
unsatisfyingly, a little primly.

I continued, 'He has had quite extensive contacts with
Bahia.'

'Not from his accent,' she said, 'but it must be reassuring
to you to have a protector.'

I had never seen Pavel in that light; an embarrassment at
times, offering to guard me against invisible, ephemeral
enemies.

'Besides,' Luisa went on, 'he can always tell us what
you're up to.' She laughed. I now saw Pavel in that light –
as a source of information about me to 'them'. But they
already knew everything. They knew Pavel's story. Too
much knowledge was flowing. What seemed to be lacking
were people stupid enough to believe it all. Or perhaps, after
all, it required intelligence to absorb it, suck at it till the
little kernels of truth, tasting of cinnamon, popped out, like
those sweets from Ecuador, whose centres at times are truly
amazing.

'This looks like a donkey-park. Or perhaps a place where
lovers cut up their partners' bodies before throwing them in

the garbage.' Luisa is in her mood where coldness tweaks out a laugh, censure can't resist a compliant grin. Pavel and I look like two footpads in an old etching who have lured the queen of Naples among the rocks, and find themselves imaginatively too impoverished to lay hands on her. Pavel's shaved head looms ahead like a lantern wrapped in cobwebs. He lopes along with a step not learned in Prague. We seem an unlikely band to effect the reconciliation of Africa and America, under the friendly, lay aegis of Rome. Indeed, like drivers who can't stay on highways but keep lurching off onto country turnoffs, we seem impelled to go digging for roots, traces of old, rejected failures. 'It's a compulsion,' I explain to myself. But the others hear and relate it – who knows how – to their own pasts. And. then I think of Nico and his hole, Juliao and his family I now firmly believe in, in Gary. It seems everyone has a family growing up twisted but in the American grain, in Gary. I become gloomy like the others.

The fissure becomes wider. The walls glisten with saltpetre, or they may be the eyes of ancient dark-seeking insects, biro-blue like those in Juliao's minder's notebook. It is light above and dark below. There is a whirring and jostling among us – it might be little boys, or one of us stumbling extravagantly. Luisa says in a bored voice, 'One of them was a parrot. It bit my bottom.'

'Probably an ancient republican feeling lonely.'

It is a place for dividing the spoils, settling accounts, planning the assault of the city. Underfoot there are thousands of what feel like paper cartridges but instead are dusty machined pieces of wood, the length and shape of a finger. We make out hoops without barrels, large skulls without horns, leaflets for a magician in Caserta. Of military heroes, no trace. Pavel seems pleased by the discovery of an empty space, perhaps for sleeping in.

The light turns green, and we are out, halfway up a valley overlooking New Rome. Blocks of former workers' flats – some with plastic cladding beginning to peel away – are pegged regularly over the landscape. Some are white and some are the colour of Incas. Red and white cars make a complex enamel pattern between the islands of habitation. Large patches of green hold gipsy camps. It looks like an immense model of modern living in the hands of an inexpert, or perhaps malicious, child. Like the ones with electric trains who engineer pile-ups and mutilate the station-masters and porters. It seems there is no room here for Pavel's goldfish and his lover from Bahia. But then it strikes me that there is an infinity of possibility for keeping goldfish, killing lovers, even sleeping in the fields. Only seafaring is difficult: the grey-green Tiber squeezes itself round its meanders like old khaki oilpaint forced from its tube. One cannot conceive a blue sea waiting to welcome and purify it.

Pavel wants to go back. Luisa says, 'In Bahia we can imagine new people coming from the sea, colonists who will at last civilise our land. Here, it seems too late. Everyone is already here, and in abundance. They're all clotted together, like wasps. All wasp nests are alike – a feat of great brilliance, but quite chilling.'

It is hard to see if she is disappointed. After all, it is only on the stage that one can, is asked to, make magic. Bahia is not a city, it is music, and its own reflection, carnival. We can live by no other reality. Decoration keeps us alive, decor feeds us. Unable to make things with our own arms and legs we contemplate our surroundings through pretty mirrors. Luisa is unimpressed.

'But you, more than anyone, tries to make the mirrors pretty – having failed with prettifying reality.'

'I won't deny it,' I say. 'But we are the lucky ones, because we know what it all once looked like, before we started tacking on beauty everywhere, brushing off the old furniture and introducing comforts.' And indeed, perhaps that's what attracts me to Bahians, and to Pavel – the discomfort of their reality.

Luisa said, 'I can show you the kingdoms of the world. I can't give them to you, because you don't want them.'

I replied, 'They aren't yours.'

'They're no one's.'

It was true. She had nothing to give me that my freedom had not already mapped out as wasteland, or a no-go area. It was I, by risking my freedom – such as it was, call it the sum of my mistakes, anxieties and little triumphs – who stood to lose. Such judgements were unfashionable. It was assumed everyone started off the game with the same rules, the same number of tokens, but really this was part of an egalitarian myth no one took seriously until a relationship had come apart. It reassured me to think I had more to give Luisa than she at the moment had for me. She would fill empty spaces, whereas I, or my situation, represented areas already occupied and cultivated. Curiously too, she would shut off Bahia, the Bahia I imagined. And yet, there was a kind of symmetry in our uneven hopes and gifts. We were two strangers who collide and find their parcels, all mixed up, serve the other better than the original bearer.

Luisa is a statue, waiting for me a speak, caught in that incongruity for a second. A caryatid who has lost her burden and determined to support no more. A pleasant statue, like those in two contrasting colours of marble, faces black, the toga salmon, as though to tease us, knowing the face is white, the toga too.

'Well,' I say, 'we have come a long way. Should we go back?'

It is not clear to any of us what we have seen. No one has commented on the magnificently comprehensive landscape, broad as those grim skylines they engraved for tourists on the grand tour, showing Rome a forest of numbered churches, christianised obelisks. A trio of cicadas is joined by a second viola, stubbornly untuned, without a part, silenced by its own incongruousness. Luisa fits into the relative silence here, the spikes and. clusters of the pineta set her off. In Bahia she would have more physical presence, here the sky is bigger: in the West, animal shapes in the sunset clouds rear up, the rest is still three planes of baroque, clouds that presage nothing serious, except perspective.

Against her will, Luisa had seemed a figure in a landscape – one of the Roman countryside's notorious tricks, all Rome on the outer rim being made of ledges falling away to unpeopled plains, huts, a few sheep, here a brigand, there a horse in swamp up to its saddle. Promising, for me, something more personal, even a little humble – humility not for itself, but enforced by the physical setting. And always a countryside in which no one seems to do anything, to work – a background like a photographer's set of backcloths, suitable for bishops, new graduates, parachutists.

*

It was soon after this afternoon, inconclusive, that we heard from Angola. A telephone call from Juliao, both the man and the electronics horribly confused and fractured. Nico had been in an accident. 'Terribly injured ... pinned, just literally pinned together. Consciousness irreparably interrupted   ... but with a luminous lucidity a series of messages ... '

So, we could not know if he was alive or dead, if he had been injured in fighting or on the road. Luisa's first angry comment was, 'Who cares if he was drunk?' but this was part of a quicker dialogue than I could be involved in. She looked destroyed. I reasoned: being pinned implied fractures, not sudden death, coma and messages were incompatible.

In the next days, it seemed only Luisa had part of the truth. All the accounts agreed that Nico had been drunk, with the abandon I had seen in New York. But then everything was confusion – a road accident. A landmine. Or both. Or just the mine, a personnel one, perhaps put together in Italy. Improbably, the Italian ambassador was involved then fluttered out of frame. Had Nico been killed, was he dying, had he recovered and then died? Was he a martyr to the cause? Even – a suggestion Pavel and I entertained – had his 'death' resolved immediate embarrassments caused by his presence? Or had Aghassian seen him as the key figure, giving a social symbolism to the project? Had him eliminated as a pivot, if not actually a luminary. This was Luisa's idea.

I was worn down by the doubt and frustration, and the question of life and death lost its hard edge, its divide. This was limbo. Luisa, on the other hand, was in constant agitation and expectancy. She renounced everything: Bahia, New York, Angola. Only Rome gave her an edgy peace; contemplating its infinitely monumental side, she seemed to find a physical dam against the presence, or the absence, of Nico.

In times of grief, real feelings about people are of little consequence. The stasis of the project, if not its death: the wounding, or possibly the death, of its hero, placed all our existences in a precarious state. Luisa said, 'We must go on, even here, even where there is nothing to do, nothing to start from,' but it seemed a formal statement, to give herself courage, and certainly not resting on my real or potential reliability.

We had a letter from Juliao, in which only the second page arrived: '... with long steel pins. He did everything possible, and reported Nico as saying he was in a dark hole, but digging himself out, and giggling – perhaps the anaesthetic? It is a terrible period in my life, especially as we suspect the author was someone very close to us. Please let my family know of my own part in all this, it may reassure them somewhat. I hope you share my views on the future of the project. You know, incidentally, how I hate guards and all that formality. But now I have an official position, I should prefer to have people about me who are trustworthy. Pavel probably feels too well-established in Rome to come out here, but you may remember my driver in New York, who would of course be ideal given what has happened here. Do not be too downcast, and for Luisa, in the most tremendous way, this will give her the opportunity to resolve her own plans.'

To these mysteries, which seemed almost intentionally planted, I found in a review of third world revolution in the early '60s a denunciation of Carlos: 'in US and Brazilian military circles, uses his knowledge of Spanish and Portuguese political circles to gather saleable information – well-documented presence in counter-insurgency contexts, acting as "civilian" expert on local social conditions ... comrades are asked to take note of this and to make the information as widely known as possible.'

A sectarian quarrel? An incautious lecture? Part of the archaeology of movements long since reclassified, stopped moving, retransformed into powers and counter-powers.

Only with projects are there corrupters and corrupted: in regimes of anarchy or anomie everyone is both – at once mini-corrupter and slightly corrupted. No one expects pure souls, they are a nuisance, as well as suspect.

Luisa was not a pure soul, but her presence, as a corpseless widow, jarred. She clung to me more than she had ever done: rather than 'clung', 'adhered' would be better. At moments like this, when there is a partial letter to interpret, words took on more than their usual burden, and broke under the strain.

We had neglected our expedients, and were short of cash. The unusable currency lay under the fields like a feast for maggots. I did not suggest exhuming it, and did not say if I knew where it was. In any case to touch it would have been to compromise oneself, with friends and enemies of the project. We went into the countryside to gather wild chicory and plants with many names, but reduced on cooking to the same pre-cabbage aspect, a primitive, undifferentiated taste of root and leaf. Luisa proposed killing a sheep, but I said, 'The shepherds know them all, the hair on the neck is different.'

'So,' she said, 'they'll know that one is missing, certainly dead.' We dropped the subject. The landscape turned brown, the oaks metallic green. We felt like skins pegged out and splitting, hooves and horns thrown in tired piles, unusable.

The new subjectivism left me, and my neighbours, untouched. I should not have expected anything else. The scale of the operation was tiny, the incidence of the friendships Juliao wanted to extort from it, insignificant. We were not enough to make a cartoon, a mixed-mode tale reeling off like a peepshow or a panopticon with capering figures.

And yet, somewhere in the fields, the Roman field, all that money, which everyone knew about, called like one of those figures, half insect and half rodent, hopping and slithering in the backwoods of Bahia. In this, Juliao had been right – those greenbacks would cement our small universes, give us something to live and die for, and certainly a means of telling friend from nearly friend, keeping alive our various dreads, or recurrences, of jail.

12   *Luisa – Moving Time?*

ERE IN *the countryside, I feel I am in the city diluted, as if these sounds, of sheep and water, children playing in the ancient mode, are not the sounds of close life but reflections borne in. So, every day, I feel that Nico will not make it, cannot make it, as he tunnels through whatever death, whatever physical encumbrance he has, through to the streets of Bahia, with roses in his hair.*

Meanwhile, I am put incongruously in the part of the lady who has lost her little dog. He – Nico – has resolved the problem of his existence, my own things have fallen apart. Back to the earliest questions I go. Is this grief I feel for Nico? certainly impatience. Is my lover in Rome intelligent, precise? Do I want that, in any case? And surely he is not the last. And not the best.

With the project I felt I could put together different people – quite an extravagant network, complementing a weakness here, fulfilling a promise, a determination, there. And it was – kind of – beginning to work.

What use is my knowledge, my plan? I thought, 'Through art, even my art, you become bigger, more plural, other. But not other than you are. No magic, just more concentrated, limited in certain ways. By singing, not speaking, whistling not shouting, you are protected against certain excesses. You pay the price for changing time and experience, the price any magician pays for fiddling with reality, enhancing it but also traducing.'

And yet it is not another world, the magic is not real, which is why, after all, we love it without fear. It is still all the human world, full of human efforts and meanings, resisting transcendence – fortunately perhaps. Enter the painting by peering at it, make the emotion ring out through tricks in the voice.

Everyone thinks the Etruscans had some magic for survival. But I think they just gave up. Hope that death would be a grey fizzling; hibernation or cold valves sizzling with leftover current still. When there is violence in Bahia, it is a direct charge from sex and money – perhaps the Etruscans lacked enough of both. Violence is a terrible, a useless thing – but what do we get from it? Is it only useless, is engineering not also tremendous, explosive? All these Etruscan hydraulics, the necropolis as their metaphor for cities – isn't that a charge of violence misspent, directed wrong?

Like my working with, working through other people. Is there a difference? When there is stasis, I question my power. But that's because it isn't working. I like my engineering, I like my violence, because it's strong, not wanton.

My lover in Rome says he has never been **held** *by anyone before me. People keep themselves separate, for fear of being held in return, or fear of seeming violent, greedy. It's not my way. Juliao with his family, Nico in the hole, even Pavel with his stories about his lover – and my lover, persevering with his expedients: I love their striving, persistence, love giving it meaning and form. And I can. Nearly, this time. Poor Nico.*

And shall put it to work again, no more the repetition of carnival, no more Trumpet Wheel, no more plotting in bars. Rising up and up, out of Bahia, out of Brazil even. Up and up, almost all the way to Mars.

My lover here says, 'The worst thing is not to be used. To have no one who thinks you are useful – or usable.' That's what we gave him, tried to give him. Not to be a kingfisher, the flash like a crystal of salts not washed off the grey film, but to be – if necessary – someone who would kill their lover, rather than have their love, or lover, die. Me today, and you tomorrow. And today – it's Nico. Burned into me like the town he burnt for me. Or rather, it was me he wanted, and we were quite indifferent to the town. Two damned indifferent fissile atoms, dancing off like sparks through the trees. One spark, quivering out. Nico. But I am going forward, cutting the path, cutting a path through living things – a terrible, a tremendous way of moving forward. All those insects, with their sharp blue eyes, all jostled aside, the trees and fronds maybe a hundred metres tall, subsiding, slumping, all those marvels of cell, of habitation; peering at the little colonies of fur and shell, the beetles. God, could you think of just counting the beetles in the forest! A mystery of cubes and squares and roots. So many of them, as one advances, machete raised, intentions of travel, pacific, but cutting it all down, renewing, opening up the grey light into blue.

Perhaps there is no resolution, but things do finish, cannot be started or tried again. We are full of power, the fields are full of money. How does this fit in with Nico's suspended animation, my stasis with my lover? I don't know, I can't know. And again, I can know, I do know. It is cutting the path, leaving the sea behind and pushing forward into the dark – that is a terrible, a tremendous task – to cut down all that growth, to move forward over its profusion.

Poised. Rather antique. But already feeling the air begin to lift, to stir again. As in late afternoon, walking by the sea, in Bahia.

From JANICULUM

Scenario

plane lands
hot
passport, taxi,
restaurant –
at least, there's tables

it's one

dream of world food,
sugar, diced eggs
a salted snake
– in the kitchen
prayers and gunfire

and it's two

some come and go
but no one serves
although – there is a to and fro
and faces looking in

it's three

eat we must
concoct,
or snare some bird
– is it possible

that no one comes? –
or make a blaze, unless
we're wrong, and here one doesn't eat, but celebrates,
or takes exams, or tablecloths
encoded differently
are not the strip
on which we eat

it's four

of course, the morning staff
is gone:
there starts
a process of transition,
service from full to self,
and then again perhaps
a fry-up,
and at least
we've got the duty-free

it's five

better at times to stay alive
than eat –
the gunfire
is more distant now,
the faces' to and fro
is more a statement than a threat –
the cat
is not quite food
but not quite friend,
and will not serve us in the end –

it's six

I know the scratches on
the record better than the tune:
it seems it's one of mine: impossible
– in this strange town
neglect is king, no food and so
no memory, no
sugar and starches climbing up the stair, it's

time to move on

Night Flyers

half-naked dreamers, they fly – diaphanous thighs –
over the frosted, coagulated night-cities.
They fall and balance, their dark membranes
taut against consciousness, memory:
gripping the charmer's frozen tear,
they dance a happy ritual sleep, watching slime
grow on the roofs, slip to the pavements for the early cats.
Guilt, dusty bottles full of old leaves,
silver battlements: their world.

Wishful wanderers, they seldom look down:
unbalanced heights, the ivory smell of sleeping flesh,
and young, brittle fangs – these fill a fantasy.
'Bats and unholy porcupines,' cry the farmers
as the bodies kick: look, you may see them,
they will be high as willows, fast as tired brandy:
you may even see one squinting, ducking,
practising remorse.

If you are lucky, you might watch one enter
his window, squatting on thick air before the sill,
then bending glass like the mist of dreams, opening
red curtains with stars on them.

Dogs

Dog licks dog's nose – porous, continental:
tastes alum, silver pistols, goats in a cage,
blood from orange hares hooked by one leg, for sale.
Skulls filled with minerals. Lizards, chocolate;
Indians impacted like coal
asleep
     Time is trapped here, time
to run round and bestraddle
this khanate. But no – he has forgotten
the history of the leash.
And learns again.

Beginning

Discovering the wheel was easy –
pawprints into fresh gold,
even mints:
some trees changed – not uniformly –
to red: the fog one knew would lift:

discovering the gold was easy,
paws under wheels: some mints changed
– the fog, one thought, would lift:

discovering the mints was easy,
fresh gold into ice-cream bricks

discovering the paws was easy –
covered in fresh gold
and fog and leaves.

Discovering the wheel was difficult
– bogged in wet gold and leaves:
wonder is easy and hope difficult

splay the toes, plunge and burn them
in broken codes – Intelligence? Slaves certainly.

Discovering the wheel was easy
– the trees hold off
going to red, are foggy orange.
Paws black after gold,
prints (and leaves) burnt off

discovering was easy,
prints into gold,
trees into fog
wonder: hope difficult,
changed.

Sack of a City

That night we ran their own harrows
over the tessellated pavements:
struck fire from bezils and sparrows
on stones in the soft cement.
The prongs of the harrows skidded
from prelate to small partridge:
as we raked over stone, heavy-lidded
emperors winced at the iron-edge.

Rome, June 1976

'do you say "a mad heat"?' well, no, rather
'absurd' – the ruffled thrush (or pinecone)
sits in his tree – What sort?
or kind, or kindness suggests
to keep a continent open for four people,
– can't remember which country I left
my tennis racquet in – roses, today's subject:
no – off with his hands is Arrabal,
and head is Freud – excuse!
Seek that excuse for all those left behind,
oneself hung up like pyjama suits in storage
– but no, explain, the hands for masturbation
or for painting? No, for anti-fascism –
but in an afternoon we can learn roses
from 'inside-out', concrete, the names
are all of queens, rich ladies, peace –
enlarge your general knowledge; and someone wrote
'Now can we write about roses?' – roses
are here, parts named, unchanged since when
you learned that other scented language;
oak, not cypresses – 'only the landmines woke him up' –
sleeping through war to find roses all over
in different languages, the parts unchanged,
learning so slow the names of roses, rich ladies,
– it's there still, black falling in the night, and waking
to thrushes, ruffed, to roses under palm-trees.

The Beast

I am the beast, the keeper/kept,
who mustn't bite but can
with one shudder
destroy gardens:
not good or evil, key to the ape,
radical needs sent – via the key –
alone to the forest: chews trees, pisses:
at times watches humans in their
civilisation:
sometimes eats a gazelle

slowly learns the logic
and friendship of the leash,
the evening walk, lights
going out

This City Reaches to Africa

betrayal, melancholy, nostalgia,
the soft vices: underground,
stone-lit, blue and cloud fixed:
big marble faces without eyelids
bubble sulphur down their chins,
faience, majolica, palms trained
underground, all underground.
Dogs with white eyes, half-skulls
their magic sold separately or gone for good –
clawmarks, strawberries, a cherub;
silver, turquoise, hooks for mermaids
shaped like asparagus, loaded with barbs

explosive

tribute – indulgence granted
to the soft (no peace, no rest, the black seas
thrashed and clawed by half-fish) – reaching to Africa
through suburbs filled with restless artisans

giving, taking, accumulating:
betrayals betrayed a thousand times
gnawing and burning still, the hammers
tap like heartbeats in the bad dream,
fretful, memories, making the marble flowers
for empty palaces.

The Dream, '76

clumsy with words he carpentered
– many nails to fix the logs: an early house
pioneered, with too much money, all the animals
their skins dried out, the white hares trapped
incontinent: the stock original, wasted,
too many nails to fix the green logs firm,
flop the furry bodies down, then start
to say goodbye, the primal
remittance turned to water – medium of beer,
wine and rye: stocking up the bar, now
letting go, farewell, farewell –
the nails criss-crossed to make the family house,
too many nails, words to say goodbye:
clumsy with words
spent shells, tumble down the wolves –
epithalamium. Sanctus, farewell –
'the shots rang out', the biking season's here –
a nice cold beer
sweetens the word, logic tacks the logs –
remorselessly hammered ... restless for the open green

Farewell. Sanctus, farewell.

We Must Have

done wrong to end so bad:
>God was always terror,
>now masked and armed
>completes the trial.
>Kill him again,
>God of the kingdom never come,
>God of the sphincter,
>nursery rules: bang, bang.
>He suffers for our sins,
>but so do we, lambs with the wolves
>still snapping round.

started wrong, to end so bad:
>annul. Bring justice, then,
>let them all pay, all of them,
>me too, cancel out
>the nothing, dreams of running,
>morning sweats: let no man
>fear
>dismissal, prison, gun
>will come

no roll of drums,
>no cell change,
>no nature adding wrong –
>just God:
>fear Him, in the woodcut,
>down go the bankers, down
>the politicians, profs –

rest wait: fear the Lord,
        saved or damned,
        nothing was built,
        so much vanity
        for nothing: too late
        for comfort
        in decline.
God loose among the greedy men,
        they shall have nothing
        like the rest

Life in the Middle Ages

Novels are about people – they
have to be, but poems can be language-bound,
those moist angles, flooded, frozen.
The cat with the black tail, crying for my dinner –
I don't remember: nor she remember me.
The telescope is off the Belvedere,
trees, green when last I saw them, fields,
yellow and reedy, under varnish,
the sleeping empire between empires, tempera –
and what is left without the leaves, tonguelike, rustling
– a stern country, and industrial.
Resting? Winter, but for some
a hardening

Romans

tough Romans test
their mortality
through others –
'roos and narwhals,
armour of ivory, teeth
red like chessmen

lymph in black sand
guts all over

tenderness: hardly
beauty a marbled smile

there must be
moments
with cats indoors, all
anger spent, demons
down under

a less precocious
curiosity for death,

waves not breaking,
wheat where no armed men
guard

a field of flowers
where no dust brings
geraniums to the brain

no drums and horns,
just
a caress, another test

THE FIFTH SEASON

Poems from the Etruscan

Foreword

The ancient village stands on the shore of a deep volcanic lake. It has a tussle with time, and with Faustian time, time in reverse – as if you watched the wake of your aeroplane flowing backwards as you cruised forward. There are riderless horse races through the streets; at carnival the schoolchildren dress as Minnie and Mickey Mice on the floats. Circuses come and go. There is a little airport where they launched trial military planes over the lake. This is the borderland between Etruria and Rome, the Etruscans transforming the area into a vast, moist city of the dead.

The Fifth Season

martial lizards on their toes,
aloft our mercenaries benevolent:

the Mickey Mice are scattered by the wings
and cries of falling angels.

'The shortest knife, the smallest gun
if frightening's your aim',
but then, if quality's your game
your Doctor Faust is here, and there,
a line of blue across the blue,
his time runs dialectically,
the spiral up and down – banal.

But now God leaves the genocide
to us, invents our flight, earth, lizard-
ships that never land – steady,
unheeded on his screen.
Project or chaos, a straight bright line
the vital signs maybe. Just planing,
steady on the edge of brightness
as it slices through
past and to tomorrow. He's
time and its master. A time here broken,
re-ordered in the fifth,
our, season. The other country.

Etruria: October

wood under stairs
the summer fires
pass into mist:
magpie feigns a nest
the chairs outside
back into black

we don't belong
in nature, understand
the right to kill,
or species. Spider,
various, climbs up nothing
to the roof

school again, and class:
sausages for tea,
band practising:
the small white owl
is lost fumbles
down the street

Shoreline

Boat makes own shorelines, moves on, from, through it. Boat green, hard edge, cuticle green on Chinese white – water out of its element. Strata in the water – they too more colour than substance: a touch of violet, wrinkles moving, could be monsters underneath, but truly all we see is travelling gunmetal against the white. Sky too is white, fizzling out with thick drops of mist from the trees stickied by spiders. The hills make another line of white, greyer than the other whites, serrated, rocking, but if we could isolate that white from all the others – it's a white of mist and water, memories and minds of dead legionaries ticking over, idling in deep sleep, pure brain, unscanned, rest.

Boat on its own divide, between identical elements, its colour only, like a cold animal's, and movement, making distinctions, wake and landfall, in the white.

Early Fall

Lake turquoise pales to eggshell –
blue-green and chalk, around are songs
of dying airmen. Moths and worms
infest the mushrooms, green beneath.
Cat gnaws on trout's fins and its guts –
Serpent is here. Not sacred
not benign, but present,
ready for the rite, indifferent,
promiscuous to reverence.

Cat growls: eel's ears
she cannot chew
give her a mandarin air.
She cannot last a winter here:
has bitten off a surfeit and
she spits, will puke,
doesn't see the new green,
things breaking up.

Ara della Regina

of sacrifices, blood naturally
of others, fields of thistles
drunk with it; 307 prisoners
– one day, or spread over? –
fields of sacrifice.
Wind blows horribly, lifts whole slopes
– fly over, not crossing sun.
Blocks are honey, slate,
draw down the sun.
Warship of blank sensation.
Throats offered to October sun;
always unseasonable, death deferred
crops into winter. Brown chards,
thistles, broken pots.

Still Day

faded lead on white
ripples come on, when they stop
birds step on white.
Child's notebook drowned,
moved on, promoted, uncomplete,
tracks of small beasts take over:
gull moves on lake from paper
on to paper; circus comes and goes
– the youngest jugglers, finest trumpeters
move us on, promoted, even a diploma –
through the few leaves; pause and watch
gull fish through misty paper,
a single line of lead
almost makes the shore.

Horse-racing

Horse is ruined:
racing down the road
leg broke as tomb fell in –
all damp and underwater
dream invaded by the seep.
No muscles, to climb up the wall:
dreamers awakened, paddle round
in death, still all walled up,
dreams even of the gods
cut off. Last jump
of ghosts in tomb, fall back again
– the rush of air on water seals and steals
a second time: image is air on air,
pots, bracelets, olives
long just stones. Horse
breaks down privacy maintained
by cherry tree outside, figs
for forgetfulness,
a rose

S now

snow's a memory, although
lake sucked it down,
the blotted cows
had plodded it to mud:
squalls from our toy volcanoes
plunge in the waves – a proper change
of face, fields useless and pre-human
warning of cold in ditches;
cats keep company, bus skids.
Snow blocks the trip,
a memory of snow fades back to green
– a memory I'd seen from other sides,
contained: a private fall.

Airman

bloated, coming down
with magic mushroom
powered above –
eyes two freshly boiled blue
barley sugars, sucked
in the lake, breaking legs,
surface not soft at all:
kite waits on shore
fish settle back
wait
dragged down all of us

Necropolis

wet dreams let
Etruscans melt away –
a dream of dreams.
Those baked in pots, instead,
a sudden go, with hopes
of some more startling dream.
But tomb slow cool – the dream
will last for ever,
rich serene,
cats gaunt around the rocks –
a calm eternity with everything to hand
or else for slaves a spark:
race with two dreams,
pots and the flame because they knew
in tombs the rich ones rot
with everything to hand:
staked all, the cooking,
moment of truth or
end of the game.

Robbing Tombs

dip the blade a bit
clay opens an ellipse
a tomb where we shaved down the wall
is under water:
promise of gold false teeth
cups of an orgy, pizzle-pricks
of horsemen, the long trip
of psychic death, sleep which goes on
and key to sleep, bagpipes
and scrotums, wine and the chase:
death is unriddled – the dream
no longer morning-sweated, it
doesn't end, a dream in tufa
all together, safe and rich –
dream chambers, dream eternal
– wood and the wife in stone,
frizzed into peperino,
only the stone and pots
bits of the dream – the gold teeth
smiling on through happy dreams.
Mickey eternal, women at last
beside, money to spend
carousal of the mind, but quiet
await two thousand years of seepage
and the plough; a good dream stolen.

Clouds Down

of winter, nothing to be said
TILT of seasons
gulls indifferently
on sky, on water,
divided by a palm line
Etruscan smoke appears
sometime as hope of warmth,
of fish hauled out –
the cat knows better:
lights at noon,
faces red and frightened in the glass.

Drivers Insighted by the Rain

boar inedible
mashed up in back
of special garbage truck
– strong pizza smell:
prospects of flight with dying fish,
sold to a slavery not understood –
esprit de corps of gladiators,
of wayside warriors, mashed down;
of lake all occupied, fish driven out
all middling, gulls sulky.
Perhaps one day my little fish
will dive against those beaks
the clouds with claws and feathers
– no pots anonymous, no tombs
that took all winter and an industry.
Apricots, too late, tended by Medes
with love, or rather
with not too much regret.

Rain Interrupts the Vegetable Harvest

dark camera recalls absences
walking hesitantly out of frame
Latin prepared for epitaphs, ex-
patria. Languages smother,
embower, swag of officers,
wet piles of sampietrini,
clots of oft-dead things.
Dark rainy fields of chicory, kids
go hooting home to TV. A guard
like the empty deadman in his cape,
artillery uninvented, stylish exit
fades left, pen or cane
incising memoirs.
Highland mist and hills
block sunset. Were those fields
wind-burnt, just one film ago?

Retired Officers

eyes used to wandering in wider margins
civilisations bumped and scored like touching wheels
gods carried off to guard the orchards
fates planned for prisoners, spectacles,
a time for writing, and for clients,
shabby trophies, enough words for Persian slaves:
blood pudding steaming,
chopping swords and shaman's masks,
straw huts thrown down, shards of inner empires,
tarred stoppers, plumes of egrets,
languages half-learned, heavens away.
Conscience – wax tablet, sarcophagus a long stone bath.
Look out on lake:
the alien streams, bean farmers,
goose girls, penetration in cane brakes

Etruscan Cities

cities now are little ones
– the ginger donkey in plusfours
has made a store
of droppings in the chapel tower:
sheep to their pens
like figures round the clock –
the Princess tomb is gingerbread,
a plastic bag for pottery
floats on the floor.
Through limestone to the tufa
streams run two ways: rose hips and old man's beard.
Etruscans
guarded now by brambles,
shepherds in the rock
with candles – left us
a city of the dead,
a massive citadel, no huts
or palaces: tombs gutted,
evacuated. Mountains
we can't live in,
huge resurrection,
stones rolled aside or stolen
– bodies sink down through the rock.
Nettles and brambles block
the little doors,
lintels immense. Realists,
they left dead cities;
fried in pots or tired
seeping into tufa,
impress with dying,
left wooden roofs cut out in stone.

Dying Dog

hard day:
I think my paw was split
but back is worse – can't piss,
embarrassing, the people round
would sooner leave me this last day:
the visitors would have someone
with the guts to take a gun
and – here in this flowerbed –
uncivil, polish me off:
pity and piety, good friends,
– lying in my skin all broken up,
they back off me.

This last day is not without its sense,
a flowerbed, lake, last clouds,
a breeze to mend the breaks

Lake under Rain

ugly: glum gulls,
shrewd and spiteful rain
busy with itself: fire
a latent cat with devil's eyes.
The trees are half bare emperors,
mushrooms submerged, rain mottles lake
like pitted subway paint; surface
hedges its bets, drops
metered exact and will be still
when trees are trees and gulls
see clear the goldfish
– beetle makes tracks,
the rain comes in.

The Other Lake

Path runs over Etruscan tombs
stone robbers' jars
looters in turn dead for millennia.
On the hill the broccoli pickers
are doubled up. Bored horse
herds cows, the glorious bantam rules
– the primal childhood, country, fallacy.
But then there is the other lake,
below the tombs and brambles, where the track
is riven out with water:
a few gulls, in threes or plaintive,
castle and tower,
two tractors purr in spells.
The empty tombs go back
into prickly underbrush –
sort of company, need for each other.

Deaths of Lakes

just needs joining up,
the pumps and drains;
the lake may die, but never has:
was born of fire, and dips and rifts
subsiding into water:
may die a merely possible death,
born of what fires, waters,
friends of fish and birds
at battle there – below,
salts and hot water bubbling up.
Our city knows the lake
will die with troopers riding round.
Lake is body, not a pet,
but still a population,
seeks no lies.

Day Closed in by Scirocco

fish are quartered out
in nets for dying under water –
gulls follow us about,
the slow discharge of humans;
glass the third band near the shore
– age of aquariums, the other lakes
one riffed, one distant, smoky,
tacked by one sail, one windsurf
three kinds of water, discovering
Chinese whites, small meshes.

The Hunt, the Sun

pushing to summer
swifts fall to stubborn jaws
of cat:
dancing in the street to greet
the certainty of victory
Roma, Roma, Roma.
The wolves have gone,
the terrace holds its civil wars:
swift wings too perfect,
but the lizard's tail's
cut for survival
and the cat's soft mouth.

Walk Deferred

going to take the walk:
mud hides the goldfish in the lake
sun lights odd fields,
the rain which rusted everything last night
just swells the glass:
the mushroom hunt was premature –
an easy sport unless
mistake pink underside, pegleg
takes classical revenge.
The marigolds in flower,
salads of fallen leaves.
And we defer the walk,
that leads us back, the walk
where gulls fish, and little flies
surprised, leap back into the glass, and drown.

Waves and Blue

It could be the sea
mane bubbling down
on lions, or sheep.
But paint-box blue
or crimson – no need
or reference to draw the lines –
are marked on lake or sea;
nets squared off
like fish in boxes.
Relentless hammer of renewal:
gourds sacrificed again,
the sucking lambs –
they are enough to get us through.
Again the forts, the soldiers, tanks,
the fall, looked squarely in the eye –
a choice obligatory.
So many second thoughts, and comings:
memo says, seek wisdom, but on primal page
asserts its power.
Eels lost all their rights,
becoming legless too. Not rights
rule here, but blue and winds.

Epiphany

time can't remember;
incontinent, seeps in everywhere.
Ah yes, the tombs.
But Master Faustus in his leathers
guns back to childhood and beyond
before he was,
the lake fresh-formed
the eels engendering
the legend of the Serpent

is words that cannot die
and never lived

About the author

John Fraser has lived in Rome since 1980. Previously he worked in England and Canada.